CONTENT WARNING
This collection contains adult content
and is not suitable for children.

ARTIST
Luke Spooner
is the talented artist who illustrated
this collection. You can view more
of his deliciously dark work at
http://CarrionHouse.com

"The entirety of DARK WAS THE NIGHT evokes its namesake, heart-breaking, grim, and Gothic in wide-reaching sensibilities. More so, it's rich in detail, vital in history and heritage, and marks an astute triumph of literary tragedy by author Angel Leigh McCoy."
—*Eric J. Guignard, award-winning author and editor, including* That Which Grows Wild *and* Doorways to the Deadeye
(EricJGuignard.com)

"A lovely collection of poignant, thoughtful and chilling stories."
—*Yvonne Navarro, author of* AfterAge
(Facebook.com/Yvonne.Navarro.001)

"Simultaneously gritty and mythical, melancholy and powerful, McCoy's stories vary widely in style but are all evocative, compelling, and mercilessly dark."
—*Alan Baxter, multi-award-winning author of* Served Cold *and* Devouring Dark
(AlanBaxterOnline.com)

# INTRODUCTION

I'd like to address the white elephant in the room. I'm Caucasian, of Scottish descent. Some of the stories in this book have African American protagonists, and I acknowledge that I did not write them from an *own-voices* perspective. That may be a deal-breaker for some of you, but let me explain why these stories bubbled up out of me.

I moved to Virginia in 1986 and immediately felt the weight of the state's history. I'd come from Illinois, a white-bread farming state with little connection to the Civil War (that I was made aware of). Virginia, on the other hand, had ghosts.

I delved deeper into local ghost stories, and that led me to a broader study of the abominable treatment of Blacks by Whites in the South. The more I read, the more horrified I grew.

As a writer, my job—my passion—is to put myself in someone else's shoes. The writing of the stories in this book that have African American characters grew from my need to express the dread of their situations, reveal the humanity behind the characters, and share as generously as I could some of the clutching horror and shame I felt upon learning how my fellow humans had behaved.

By researching these stories, by writing them and sharing them, and by wearing those shoes for such a brief moment inside my own head, I was changed. I learned. I grew.

If you get this far but no farther, please at least take a look at the following incomplete list of Black horror and speculative fiction writers. I offer this list with respect, in an effort to boost their voices:

Marc L. Abbott

Linda Addison

L.A. Banks

Steven Barnes

Brian Barr

Chesya Burke

Octavia E. Butler

Zig Zag Claybourne

Pearl Cleage

Samuel R. Delany

René Depestre

Tananarive Due

Chikodili Emelumadu

Akwaeke Emezi

Jewelle Gomez

Dicey Grenor

Virginia Hamilton

James Haskins

Alexis Henderson

Jennifer Hillier

Nalo Hopkinson

Yawatta Hosby

Justina Ireland

Tish Jackson

N.K. Jemisin

Tenea D. Johnson

Michelle R. Lane

Victor LaValle

Violette L. Meier

Toni Morrison

Walter Mosley

Kenya Moss-Dyme

Nzondi

Nnedi Okorafor

Nuzo Onoh

Suyi Davies Okungbowa

Helen Oyeyemi

Dia Reeves

Evie Rhodes

Maurice Carlos Ruffin

Nisi Shawl

Rivers Solomon

Sheree Renée Thomas

Steven Van Patten

LaShawn M. Wanak

Wrath James White

Kenesha Williams

L. Marie Wood

K. Ceres Wright

Skip to the back of this book for other resources you may find interesting.

# Dark was the Night

A collection of short Horror works
by Angel Leigh McCoy

♦

"Dark was the night, cold was the ground
On which my Lord was laid;
His sweat like drops of blood ran down;
In agony he prayed."

In 1927, American musician Blind Willie Johnson recorded a gospel-blues song he'd written called "Dark was the Night, Cold was the Ground." Fifty years later, in 1977, the National Aeronautics and Space Administration (NASA) launched two unmanned probes into space—Voyager 1 and 2. The probes each carried a phonograph record with sounds and music from our world, just in case they encountered intelligent life. Blind Willie Johnson's recording was included as the ultimate expression of human loneliness. The song evokes the exact ambience of suffering that accompanies me whenever I write Horror. You can listen to it on Youtube.

http://angelmccoy.com/blog/darksong

# Oral Tradition

My granny had only two teeth, in the front, on the bottom. They sat crooked, pitted and decaying, and her lips fell inward, into the chasm of her mouth. Faded and splotchy, her black face had the contours of a dried-apple doll, molded with a bulbous nose. She had eyes like drops of molasses swimming in bloody egg-whites, and her skin matched her home-made dress, a wrinkled sac without enough meat to fill it.

Once, when I was very small, I asked her why she had only two teeth.

Granny replied, "Honey, I ain't got enough room for all them teeth. There's too many stories in here. They done pushed all my other ones out." She put a seasoned finger in her mouth, tapped the dual bits that remained and added, "These two, they're the only ones that matter."

My granny knew so many folktales. Something always reminded her of one: an old tree or the railroad tracks, a thunderstorm or the hoot of an owl. "Girl," she began so many times, with her earth-husky voice, "did I ever tell you the story about...." When

Granny told a story, she licked her two teeth. She sucked at them, making wet, slurping noises that punctuated her accounts of castrations, eviscerations and lynchings.

Granny wasn't the first storyteller in our family. The tradition goes back many generations. My great-great-great-grandmother arrived on a slave ship from Africa. Purchased and given a Christian name by a Virginia plantation owner, she worked in the to-bacco fields until the end of the Civil War when her husband built a church and took up preaching. She started the tradition and passed it on to her daughter, who passed it on to her daughter, and so on. The stories have come down through the family.

After the Emancipation, most of my ancestors left Virginia and moved to Ohio where they joined self-sufficient, Negro communities, initially founded by manumitted or escaped slaves to serve as stops on the Underground Railroad. Only the storytellers remained in Virginia, in the Blue Ridge Mountains where the yarns originated and where the ghosts still haunted.

Technically, the storyteller badge should have fallen to my mother, Granny's only child, but Mama never wanted anything to do with it. Born in 1948, Mama matured during the 60s, in an era during which people rejected tradition in favor of instant pleasure, social upheaval, and political rebellion. Mama wanted to travel, smoke dope, and focus on creating her own story. She wanted out of Pulaski, out of the mountains and out from under her heritage. Her marriage, in 1966, to my father, rescued her from the country lifestyle. He took her to New York, and I was born several years later.

Granny always knew that my mother wouldn't accept the responsibility. One day, many years ago, when I was barely thirteen, I was sitting at Granny's kitchen table. Granny was standing over me, picking a tick from my head. She said, "Child, it's gonna be you some day, the one who tells the stories. You're gonna have to think about that. Your mama don't want to do it, but somebody's got to. If we lose the stories, we lose our past, and that just ain't right."

Granny's yarns had a spooky, back-woods feel, but then she had come from the back woods and rarely left them. She did, however, like to brag about how she had once traveled from her home in Pulaski County to visit the big city of Richmond, previously the Confederate capital. Her daddy had taken her there to see the battlefields where his father and uncles had fought and died to free the slaves. She left Pulaski only one other time. The day my mama gave birth to me, Granny rode a Greyhound bus all the way to New York City. Otherwise, if we wanted to see

Granny, we had to go to her.

After I turned eight, I spent two weeks, every summer, at her Appalachian farm. Staying with her was a child's dream. She and I baked cookies. We played cards. We hunted sponge mushrooms for frying and wild manroot for Granny's tonic. We watched the deer and wild turkey on the ridge and listened to the mountain lions calling out to each other.

Of course, it had its bad points too. Granny refused to modernize the farm. We used an outhouse for lack of indoor plumbing. I hated hanging my bottom over that black hole with its spiders and foul smells. We cooked on a wood stove and washed in a basin. At night, we did everything by kerosene lamp.

Once in a while, Granny and I killed a chicken for our dinner. I'll never forget the time that the headless fowl jerked away from Granny in its death throes. It fell to the ground and came straight at me, straight for me, flapping and flopping. Its severed neck spattered blood all over the pen. I ran, screaming, all the way to the house. Granny laughed and laughed with her two teeth. She had to show me the very limp, very dead chicken before I would come out again. I helped pluck the carcass, enacting my own bit of revenge, and got my fingers all sticky with blood, feathers and mites.

My fondest memories revolve around the nights

when Granny told me ghost stories. We crawled into the creaky old bed, under the heavy quilts, me in my flannel pajamas and Granny in her white nightie. She tucked us in, and we settled down. Then, she told me tales. The mountain winds rattled the windows and whistled in the attic, accompanying her intense, scratchy narrations. If Granny's stories frightened me too much, if I cried or had a nightmare, she held me close and made me feel safe again. In retrospect, maybe that's why I loved them so much. They put drama and mystery into an urban child's otherwise-structured life.

Granny always spoke as if she had actually witnessed every event, and, in my childish ignorance of time periods and Granny's age, I believed she had. My favorites included the ghost that haunted the Lyric Theater. A mob of white men stabbed him to death the night he planned to propose to his sweetheart. Another involved a slave that had escaped from Monticello, only to find himself in the hands of several whites who recognized him. They chained him to their wagon and beat him, then made him walk all the way back to his master and their reward. When he couldn't walk any more, they dragged him. The slave died. Near the railroad tracks, on dark nights, the clanking of his chains and the hopelessness of his sobs still carry through the woods, according to

Granny.

Knowing what the stories meant to Granny, and knowing that I was just one in a long line of story-tellers made me feel important, and I vowed that, no matter what, I'd carry on the tradition. Time passes, however, and as I got older, I grew away from my heritage. With adulthood came college and boy-friends, marriage, divorce and a career that pulled me away from my family. I moved to Washington D.C., joined the hordes of executive assistants in their black suit-dresses and their tennis shoes. I quit visiting Granny as often and forgot many of the stories she had told me. I tried to write a few of them down, but I confused them or lost details such as names and places.

Then my granny died. The funeral weighed upon me, as if a thousand people had died, not just Granny. I had to make peace with myself over the lost oral tradition. I told myself it wasn't my fault, that Granny, damn it, should have written those stories down, or gotten me to transcribe them for her. In the weeks that followed, I made a renewed effort to document what I could, but despite the many, many nights I had spent listening wide-eyed to Granny's stories, I could only remember a few. I vowed to contact my mother, as soon as I found time, and pick her brain for all the little details I couldn't remember. Surely, she had some recollection of the stories. Surely.

Then my mother died.

She went to bed one night and never woke up. Heart attack. My daddy said she hadn't been sleeping well since Granny's funeral.

After we buried my mother, after the parade of kind smiles and the offerings of home-made cake, the memories and the black lace, the hugs and the hand-shakes, I was glad to go home. The nightmares start-ed shortly thereafter. In my dreams, I ran through never-ending forests. Branches caught at my clothes and scratched me. Faces, elusive and intense, peered out of the shadows. Voices called to me; I heard my name whispered in a thousand timbres. One morn-ing, I awoke in a cold sweat. Images from my dreams followed me through my normal activities, preyed on my mind all day.

I went for a drive, trying to shake the specters. Thoughts of history and ancestral connections, my own cosmic place in the universe, haunted me as I sped down I-81 through the Shenandoah Valley. I ended up on the Blue Ridge Parkway with its pan-oramic views and communities older than the United States. A short drive turned into a five-hour medita-tion. It got dark. I found myself in Pulaski County.

Rather than drive all the way home, I decided to stop by Granny's farm and make sure no one had disturbed anything. Granny had left the farm to me, along with the thirty acres of land surrounding it, including the family cemetery in the corner of the lot. I hadn't decided what I planned to do with the place, and I hadn't been back since the day of Granny's funeral. When I arrived that night, the place felt too quiet—without Granny.

Flashlight in hand, I searched the rooms. The roving light put everything in tunnel perspective, pinpointing moments in time and disconnected pieces of history. I felt uneasy, so I lit a couple of oil lamps. The homey, familiar glow eased my tension.

The farmhouse smelled musty. I opened some windows to air it out. The hearth held a pile of burned logs and ash. I swept it. Guilt made me clean and straighten Granny's things. Her mementos cluttered shelves: vases and photographs, trinkets and china, and the musket balls we had gathered up by Mountain Lake. Her thimble collection lurked in a shadow box near the chimney. She had made the crocheted afghan spread across the back of the couch.

Bits of me roosted here and there as well. My school photos stood in neat rows upon the mantelpiece, a collage of my childhood, wallet-sized mingled with eight-by-tens, bad haircuts, missing baby-teeth, and embarrassing fashions. The plaque I had made for Granny, my six-year-old hand-print cast in plaster and painted dirty gold, hung on the wall behind the armchair.

The cuckoo clock in the hall struck ten. I dreaded the drive back to town, down those long and windy country roads in the dark. I decided to spend the night.

I settled on the couch, comfortable, with my notebook and pen, prepared to make some notes for work. A cool breeze whiffled through the lace curtains, carrying with it the aroma of magnolia. I thought of Granny telling me to peel a couple of potatoes. In my mind, I saw her offer me the cookie-dough spoon for licking. I heard the click-click, shuffle-click of her shoes as she crossed the floor.

The temperature dipped, and I pulled the knitted afghan, a hodge-podge of faded color, down over my legs. I closed my eyes—just for a moment—and must have dozed off. I found myself in a nebulous place where there were eyes watching me, white eyes in black faces.

The front porch creaked. I awoke. Suddenly wide awake, I listened intently, unsure whether I had actually heard anything or not. The lamps had burned down and let the shadows creep out of their corners. My heart pattered.

The knob turned on the front door. I scrambled to my feet. My notebook fell to the floor with a thud.

The door opened. I watched it swing inward toward me.

"Who's there?" I called. "Who is it?" I looked around for a weapon and found only the lantern. My hand shook as I reached for it.

A figure stood at the threshold, a black form silhouetted against the darker black of the night outside. I saw the hem of her dress rippling in the air flowing into the house. She stood there, head bowed, arms hanging loose at her sides. I could tell she was small and frail, perhaps elderly. I relaxed slightly.

"Can I help you?" I asked. "Were you a friend of my grandmother's?"

The woman lifted her head. Her dark eyes shone like marbles.

My heart accelerated.

A wave of darkness followed her to the edge of the dim circles of light cast by the oil lamps. I told myself I must be mistaken, but then she sucked on her two front teeth.

My granny had come looking for me, in her funeral dress, an odd combination of bloating and shrinkage. Mud covered her bare feet.

"Child," she said, in my head rather than in my ears. "I knew ya'd come." Her mouth didn't move. She shuffled further into the room and looked around at her things. Something alive moved in her hair.

"It's cold on the other side, child," Granny said into my mind. She sounded as natural as if she'd just walked in from feeding the chickens. "I need to be moving on."

I thought maybe I was dreaming.

"Now that your mama's dead, the tradition passes on to you."

I tried to wake up.

Granny caressed her dirty, blue-white fingers over a Norman Rockwell statuette. She tapped a thick, cracked and yellowed nail against the face of an antique Aunt Jemima bottle. Her voice sounded in my head, "I'm sorry about your mama, but...well, there's a lot more at stake here than her fancy cars and theater tickets. A lot of people were counting on her. She always was a selfish, weak child."

Heavy footsteps crossed the verandah and approached the front door. Momentarily, a tall, thick-muscled black man entered the room. He wore the attire of a blacksmith from the 19th century, including the heavy leather apron. His image shifted in the breeze, like laundry hung out to dry, but upside-down, with inverted gravity, anchored by his feet to the floor. Around his neck, he had the unmistakable mark of a rope burn.

I stumbled back, back into an end-table. Clumsy, I placed it between me and my visitors.

Others followed. Granny greeted them all as if they were old friends. They wore varied clothing, some ragged, some elegant, but all from a lost time, the nineteenth or early twentieth century. The most modern came from the Depression Era. I recognized many of them from the stories Granny had told me.

A young woman entered. Little remained of her dress, just patches, here and there, melted to her. Her arms crossed her chest where fire had frozen them, had cooked the meat, sinew and muscle into hard bundles. She had no hair. The flames had split and charred her skin. I couldn't tell whether she had been black or white while alive. In death, she was black as char. Her eyes had welded shut and her mouth slashed strangely across her face, too wide, torn.

Another man followed her, a Union soldier, black. His arm hung out-of-socket at the shoulder, wrong, and his knees crooked backwards. Cuts, bruises and lumps covered his face, and the stump of his tongue showed in his gaping mouth. Blood drained over his bottom lip, dripping off his jaw with the regularity of a leaky faucet. A second mouth opened wide at the back of his neck. The slash through his muscle dropped his head into a perpetually obedient bow.

Two white women arrived, dressed in peach, ante-bellum gowns. Twins, they had dark, dark eyes that glistened like those of a crow. Their hair flowed down past their waists, swaying in an ethereal draft. They seemed unmarked, but as they approached, I noticed that one of them showed the swell of pregnancy. The smell of almonds, oversweet and ripe, accompanied them. I had heard their story, from Granny. Their own father, upon learning that they had lain with slaves and that one carried the child of her black lover, had poisoned them with arsenic.

A young boy, mulatto, ran into the room and climbed up onto the couch. His nose sat crooked, broken, and his jaw dangled uncontrollably. One side of his head had a crusty indent, broken bits of skull and folds of brain showing where someone had bludgeoned him. He crouched and waved at me.

I swayed, dizzy, and leaned back against the wall to keep from collapsing.

More came, more and more. Children and adults, men and women, black and white, they piled in and turned to watch me, whispering to one another. They filled the house, the porch and the lawn. They crowded around the windows. None of them had much physical substance, their ghostly countenances all the more disturbing for the way they shifted and moved, stretched and rippled. Only Granny still had her body.

Suddenly, they grew silent, all on cue, alert and waiting. I couldn't breathe in the confining space, trapped there with all those ghosts, all those stories. A sense of anticipation crowded me.

"Your mama," mind-whispered Granny. "...rejected us, our stories, and her inheritance. It's up to you now. All these...." She indicated the specters in the room, those pressed tight to the threshold and those hanging outside the windows. "All these stories got to be told. We ain't nothing if we ain't got no past, no history. No, they ain't pretty, but that's who we were and who we don't never hope to be again."

The sound of my own blood rushed in my ears like a river cut loose from a dam. I looked around at all those miserable faces, at all the victims of murder, negligence, prejudice, and injustice. Their stories, told in the guise of folktales, embodied all the ugliness of our past. I had stopped believing Granny's stories. I had come to think they were just interesting tales meant to frighten children and pass the time. Face to face with them, however, I couldn't ignore them. That, in some strange way, affected me more deeply than standing in the company of my dead grandmother.

"You're the last of the line, child. You ain't going to have no babies. But that's okay. It's time to put it all down on paper, just like you said, for future generations. You're the only one who can do that now. Will ya do it, girl?" Her voice echoed, and others joined in on the chorus, "Will ya...will...will ya...will ya...will...will...ya?"

I put my hands over my ears, "Yes! Yes!"

The stories breathed a sigh of relief. Their whispers rippled outward around me as if I were a pebble dropped into the pool of the afterlife.

"Bless you, child," Granny thought at me.

Slowly, I lowered my hands.

With crawling, dry fingers, Granny began to dig inside her lips. She removed a plastic guard the mortician had placed there to give her mouth a more natural contour. Her lips sank inward without the support. Then, she inserted the fingers of both hands between her gums. She tugged downward on her jaw. It resisted.

"Granny?" I gasped.

Suddenly, the pin that kept her jaw closed pulled free from the roof of her mouth. The sound of cracking cartilage made me cringe. The ghosts shivered. A steel wire flopped out across her lips and bobbed there, still attached below her swollen tongue. A piece of gray flesh clung to the pin at the wire's end. Granny turned her yellowed, filmy eyes upon me and worked her jaw up and down. Those two teeth, with their rotten, black cores and brownish stained surfaces, did a morbid dance as Granny flexed muscles unused for several weeks.

I stared, frozen.

Granny then reached into her mouth and took hold of one of her teeth. She pulled. The rotted thing emerged from its fleshy pocket with a wet "squitch."

My stomach churned, and I covered my mouth. Tears blurred my vision. "Granny," I pleaded, tearing my eyes from the sight, "I've got to get out of here." I rushed headlong into the crowd of ghosts and headed for the door. I had to get out. I had to get home. I had to wake up. But the ghosts clutched at me. They refused to let me pass. They blocked my path and held me back.

I found myself lifted off the floor, arms out, legs spread, immobilized by a dozen or more hands. They turned me back toward Granny. I struggled to no avail.

"Granny! I said I'd do it!"

Granny came toward me, both teeth in her hand. An ooze of pink fluid drooled out of her mouth and down her chin. "You can't go yet," Granny said, not unkindly. "I got to give you your inheritance." Her eyes had a cold intensity, a purpose that extended beyond the grave. She grabbed my jaw with her cold, fleshy hand and tried to force it open. While living, she had been strong, but dead, her strength had doubled.

I screamed.

Granny dropped the teeth down my throat.

I felt them catch in my esophagus. I coughed. I choked. I nearly vomited. The world slipped sideways, spinning out of control.

◆

I awoke in bed, Granny's bed. The quilts lay heavily upon me, trapping me in comfort, warmth and the smell of my own sweat. My mouth tasted of last night's coffee left to ferment; my limbs felt sore and stiff. Slowly, I peeked out from under the covers. A stream of sunshine flowed in through the window and across the floor. The lazy creaking of branches and the fresh scent of honeysuckle coated me in familiarity. I was alone.

I lay there, for a long while, remembering my nightmare. I cursed my subconscious and mentally kicked myself for getting spooked. I thought about how I had let Granny down. Lying there in her bed, the past felt so far away. I considered how little I knew about my mother, about Granny, and about my ancestors. They had lived lifetimes. They were young once. They had loved, hurt, laughed, worked, and every single moment of it had meant something to them. All through the centuries, all those people, lost, gone, forgotten. Their stories died with them,

and they became nothing more than cardboard car-
icatures and names on gravestones. Already, I had
forgotten events from my own life, and when I died,
it would all fade into nothingness.

Eventually, the call of nature prodded me out of
my lethargy. I got up, dressed and walked to the outhouse. The day held the gentle warmth that comes
with Spring, so tentative and glowingly sensual. Dew
clung to my shoes and dampened the hems of my
pants. I opened the door with the moon cut into it and
ducked under a spider web. Inside, the cool darkness
enfolded me. Two slivers of light made it possible to
see. One broke through a crack in the ceiling and the
other filtered in through the half-moon. It landed on
my chest when I turned around, marking me with a
crescent.

I lowered my pants and sat on the white seat
Granny had installed over the hole. Sounds echoed
inside the outhouse, the flow of my waters and the
splash of my feces. A sudden pain in my bowels made
me flinch. I continued, careful, fearful and concerned.
Finally, nothing remained to excrete. I found blood
when I wiped.

Returning to the house, I tried to convince myself I was fine. I pumped water into a pan and heated it on the wood-stove. I poured it into a large, ce-
ramic bowl. Dipping my hands in the hot water, I

splashed my face with it. I splashed again, and again, then scrubbed with Granny's Ivory soap. Washing around my lips, I noticed a tenderness in my jaw. I let my tongue wander, sensing, feeling the inside of my mouth. I had lost a tooth. The hole lay open and sore. As I poked around in the wound, the tooth next to it loosened and tumbled into the folds beneath my tongue. I spit it and a gob of blood into the basin.

More teeth succumbed to the hysterical pressure of my tongue and fingers. I lost another. And then another. The water turned pink, then scarlet, with swirling blood and spit. The white pearls gathered in a pile with their legs and their rippled heads. Before long, they had all fallen out. All but two. I had only two teeth, in the front, on the bottom. When I licked at them, my mind filled with memories of torture and death, betrayal and sorrow, blood and sweat, Black and White, North and South.

———◆◆———

# Crack o'Doom

The sky grew ominous and cast a gloom on the farm. Jeanie's mom had told her not to leave the yard. "There's a storm comin', kiddo. Stick close." The smells of imminent rain and eager pine mingled. The leaves on the oak trees turned up, thirsty and ready.

"Storm comin'," seven-year-old Jeanie told the dogs through the tall fence. She entered their pen, careful to close the gate behind her. Daddy's labradors, Sissy and Sassy, were excited. Their tails wagged their thick bodies, and their chocolate snouts snuffled her all over.

The dogs had run down any grass that might have once grown there. They'd dug around, looking for moles and buried bones. Mangy-furred tennis balls lay strewn amidst chew-toys missing appendages and ears, and there was an old red kickball to one side, half-deflated.

Jeanie set her doll, Dolly, to one side and got down on her hands and knees at the entrance to the doghouse. She pulled out the two woolen blankets, bringing a flow of dirt and dog-hair with them. She stood and shook out the first one. It tossed up a cloud of fur and dust, and the wind blew it at her. She turned her face away—eyes, nose and mouth scrunched together.

She folded the blankets in uneven squares and put them back inside the doghouse, pressing their edges into the corners and smoothing them as flat as they'd go.

The first big blast sounded. *Boom!*

Jeanie froze in place, and her heartbeat accelerated. "Crack o'doom," she said. Jeanie's Daddy had taught her to say that whenever she heard thunder. He had said it would keep her safe.

On her hands and knees, inside the doghouse, she crawled to the entrance and peered out. The dogs had stopped playing and were watching the main house. Jeanie looked, too, at the big, white farmhouse where she lived with her parents.

Sissy let out a bark, and then a long broken yowl—the sound Mama called singing.

*Boom!*

"Crack o'doom."

The thunder was in the house.

Jeanie grabbed Dolly to her and hunkered down inside the doghouse. She called the dogs, and when they came rushing in, she burrowed between their warm, wiggly bodies, letting them push at her with hard noses, clawed paws, and lapping tongues.

A man shouted Jeanie's name. It was Mr. Conti.

Jeanie went still, head cocked to one side, listening.

"Jeanie! Your mother wants you to come inside!"

"It's Mr. Conti," Jeanie said, but she stayed put. "Shhhhh."

"Jeanie!" The man approached the dog pen. The legs of his one-piece jumpsuit, torn at one thigh and stained at the knees, came into view. He stood just outside the pen, turning in place, with the barrel of his shotgun sticking down and out in front of him.

The dogs poked their heads out. One of them growled.

"Jeanie! Come home, girl! Right now!" Mr. Conti sighed loudly.

Jeanie hugged Dolly tighter. She had never liked Mr. Conti. He watched her. He made her feel shy and unsettled. She did her best to avoid being alone with him and never spoke to him.

Sassy launched herself out of the doghouse and ran straight toward Mr. Conti. She slammed into the fence and barked up a ruckus.

Mr. Conti jumped back. "Damn dog!" He raised the gun and pointed it at Sassy, looking down the barrel at her with his mean face. He pushed the gun at her, as if firing, then lowered it. He huffed and headed off toward the woods, toward his own farm.

Jeanie's stomach eased. She didn't hear any more thunder. She grabbed her doll and crawled out. She opened the gate enough to slide out without the dogs coming with her, and she crossed the lawn to the front of the house. She went inside, careful to close the door behind her, so the flies wouldn't get in. Standing in the main foyer, she listened for her parents. Most days, she could hear where they were.

That day, however, the house had stopped—stopped breathing, stopped living. A silence had settled on the rooms, the kind that's waiting for you when you first come home from vacation, or when you wake up to find yourself all alone. It was the kind of silence that a person would do anything to chase away, like whistling, stomping booted feet on the mat and calling out to anyone who will answer.

"Mama?" Jeanie went to the kitchen, but no one was there. The TV in the living room was switched off. "Daddy?" Nuzzling her face in Dolly's hair, she crept upstairs.

She found them. In their bedroom. Mama and Daddy were lying on the floor, eyes open, staring up at the ceiling, forever. And, there was blood.

More than anything else, the smell in the room

brought tears to Jeanie's eyes. It was the smell of blood and dissipating warmth mingled with toilet and something bitter, like firecracker smoke.

Jeanie went to her mom. "Mama?" She got no response. "Mama!" Nothing. Her heart pounded in her chest, and her breath became the ragged fluttering of a frightened bird. When she crossed to her dad, she slipped in some blood, but managed not to fall. She crouched at his head. "Daddy?" He didn't move. She rocked back and forth on her feet, hugging Dolly to her chest.

The disrupted silence settled back down upon the house.

Jeanie wanted help, an adult, 911, anyone. Leaving bloody footprints on the wood floor, she went to the bed-side table, picked up the phone, and put it to her ear. She pressed the numbers—9 1 1—but the phone was silent too. Dead.

She'd seen blood before, when she'd skinned her knee, and when her mother had cut herself with a kitchen knife, but never had she seen so much blood. It had splattered the wall and made a big mess all around her parents. It pooled in the pits of their bellies and drained into cracks between the floorboards around them.

The dogs started barking again. Jeanie went to the window and looked down at them.

Mr. Conti had returned. He no longer had the shotgun, but his mouth had shrunk into a thin line, and his eyes had grown sharp and searching.

Instinct gave Jeanie a harsh push. She grasped Dolly by the hair and ran down the back stairs. She left the house through the kitchen door and stumbled out into the backyard. Her eyeballs were pushing forward, as if trying to escape ahead of her, and her breath came in catches and stops. She ran instinctively, cut through the woods, along the path her Daddy had made, and on into the kick-ball field. It started to rain, not nicely, but with all the mean intentions of a water balloon dropped from on high.

The squall came out of nowhere and crashed into the coast with a violence that bowed ancient pines and flattened tall grasses. Rain crashed down on Jeanie. It pounded her and drenched her clothes. Hugging Dolly to her, she lowered her head and sprinted to the trees on the far side of the clearing. She took shelter under a Douglas fir.

A bolt of lightning streaked from sky to ground, casting everything in blue-white light and making Jeanie's hair tingle. The flash burned white treetops onto a black sky behind her eyelids. Thunder came next, a physical blast of sound. She cringed, threw her hands up to her ears and tucked her elbows in tight against her body.

"Crack o'doom."

Little rivers of rainwater made their way across pine needle valleys and flooded the ground beneath the tree. Jeanie's tennis shoes—her first-grade shoes, now play shoes—squished when she shifted her weight.

Dolly's hair had droplets of water clinging to it. It was scrunched up and messy. Her dungarees were drenched. Her blue, sparkle eyes stared at Jeanie's chest, and her smile didn't waver. Jeanie tipped Dolly, and the doll's eyes rolled closed.

From her foxhole beneath the moisture-laden branches, Jeanie watched the rain. The drops hit the ground so hard they bounced.

The dogs gave great baying cries and deep woofs. Jeanie heard the dogs' barks in between the rumblings of the clouds.

Something crashed through the trees, and Jeanie looked to see who it was. "Sally!" she cried.

An ogre of a man named Sally, Mr. Conti's son, stopped, bent over and blinked with round, uncomprehending eyes at Jeanie. After a moment, he got down and crawled into her sanctuary with her. He sat back on his full rump, ignoring the ground's wetness, and brushed his hands together to wipe away pine needles and mud.

"There's thunder in my house," Jeanie said.

"She has to come home." Sally tugged on her sleeve.

The Contis had known Jeanie since before she was born. She had many memories, and her parents had even more, of evenings spent with the two families together. The grown-ups had played cards, read books aloud, made recipes in the kitchen or worked in the garden. Sometimes, they just talked about magick and rituals.

Sometimes Mrs. Conti would babysit her, and sometimes Mama would babysit Sally.

Sally—his mom called him Salvatore—was physically much older than Jeanie, but his mind had stopped maturing at around seven years old. He'd been born different, and though Jeanie's mom had said, "That's not a bad thing," it meant he went to a special school, and nobody in the neighborhood wanted to play with him. She was his only friend, mostly because their parents were friends. Lately, she had begun to feel the weight of it. He followed her and wanted to know everything she was doing. Before, when she was little, it hadn't mattered so much, but she was getting to be a big girl, seven-and-a-half years old, and Sally was still a little boy inside. He wanted to watch kid shows, play kid games and read kid books. Jeanie had started to feel superior to Sally, to feel bothered by his constant presence and non-growing ways, to feel frustrated by his lack of even a single original thought.

Sally was soaked to the bone. He reached out with his big, man hand to stroke Dolly's wet hair. He had given her the doll for her seventh birthday.

"I didn't know it was going to rain when I left," Jeanie said.

"I didn't know it was going to rain," Sally said.

"You're soaked. Go home. Your mom and dad are gonna be mad."

"I know." But he didn't move. He just sat there, rocking himself, hands clasped and wringing. "She has... to come home." Sally blinked his large, little-boy eyes against the water on his lashes.

"No, I can't! Your dad did something to my Mama and Daddy."

Sally shook his head. He reached down to touch the muddy, socked foot.

The sky flashed, and another blast of thunder split the air.

"Crack o'doom!" Jeanie's eyes filled with tears. She swiped her arm across them.

Sally hunkered, hands clutching his ears, body rocking, full lips trembling.

Jeanie looked over at him. "Say it, Sally."

He was confused, eyes bright, rounded head moving without purpose.

Jeanie fisted her hand in the collar of his shirt. "Say it."

"Say it," he said.

"No. Say 'crack o'doom.' You have to say it every time it thunders, or something bad will happen."

Sally said, "Crack o'doom."

"Good. Now, go home. It'll be okay."

"I know." Sally tipped his head to look out and up at the roiling clouds. "It's worth the sacrifice."

Lightning struck again. Close. This one lingered, its tail captured by something. It sucked oxygen out of the air and made a resounding crack that left Jeanie's ears ringing. She cried out, though the thunder swallowed her voice. Her vision swam with electric dots. "Crack o'doom."

In the void following the lightning bolt, the dogs' barks called out again. Jeanie jerked her face in their direction. She easily imagined the dogs, racing back and forth at the fence, digging the rut deeper with each pass, kicking muddy splatters onto themselves and each other, eyes and noses searching—searching for her. They would protect her.

She easily imagined herself, safe from the storm, cuddled into their doghouse with them, huddled under their dog-smelling blankets, warm and drying. She could live with them forever.

She steeled herself, clutched Dolly to her chest,

and crawled out from under the tree. She took off—full-bore—out into the open field, toward the sound of the dogs.

"The window is closing!" Sally called after her.

Within three steps, Jeanie lost a shoe. She stepped before she realized it was gone, and her socked foot came down in the wet grass. She stumbled to a stop, lifted her foot and hopped. The shoe had remained stuck in mud, somewhere behind her.

"My mom and dad are gonna be mad!" Sally shouted from under the Douglas fir.

Jeanie went back for the shoe, her shoe-less foot on tiptoe. She couldn't see for the water rushing down her face. With one hand, she wiped her eyes. The rain drenched her windbreaker. The nylon clung to her arms, and the hem drained low and heavy at her thighs. Rivulets ran into the neck, streamed down her back and soaked her play pants. She tugged at the weighted pants and scanned the ground, looking for her shoe.

"It's worth the sacrifice!"

Jeanie ignored him.

Another bolt of lightning came to earth. It caught a tree further along, on the ridge overlooking the clearing where Jeanie searched. Out of the corner of her eye, she saw the bolt travel down the trunk, splitting it open as it went. Pine needles exploded outward, a firecracker of sparks, quickly dampened by heavy raindrops. After the initial clap, a sizzle lingered.

Jeanie crouched, making herself as small as possible. "Crack o'doom."

Sally shouted, "My boy will be normal!"

A moment passed, then two, and then Jeanie exploded out of her crouch and ran, shoe abandoned, Sally abandoned. She bolted across the clearing, heading back to the dogs. She raced toward the tree-line.

Jeanie heard pounding footsteps behind her, joining her in flight, and she was Bambi fleeing the fire with all the other animals, intent only on reaching safety.

Sally swept up behind her, clamped both his arms around her waist and lifted her off the ground.

Her equilibrium took an abrupt shift. She flailed. Dolly went flying. Instinctually, Jeanie latched onto Sally's arm.

He crashed on toward the tree-line. Once there, he stopped and set Jeanie on the ground.

Jeanie looked up into his gasping, crazed face. "Sally! Leave me alone! Go home!" The tree overhead diluted the downpour, and she wiped her soggy hair out of her eyes. She took stock of herself and realized she no longer had Dolly. A flash of panic sent her spinning in place, peering all around her, tugging Sally so she could search behind and around him. "Where's Dolly?"

Sally looked out at the open field, at the place where he'd caught Jeanie up in his arms. She followed his gaze, and without hesitation, ran back out into the field, into the downpour, into the storm.

Sally made a swipe at her.

Jeanie ran with single-minded purpose.

The rain assaulted her.

She searched, eyes wild.

A branching bolt of lightning and its thunder cracked the sky, and the bleaching light put a shine on Dolly's face. Jeanie saw the doll. It lay face-up, spread-eagle, eyes closed, awash with rain.

She ran to her doll, picked it up under the armpits and hugged it to her heart.

Lightning struck. It connected with a nearby tree, coursed down it with white-hot fury, and sent its blaze arcing across to where Jeanie stood. It entered through her shoulder and rocketed down through her body. It expanded and filled her, wrenched her insides and twisted her brain as if it were wringing out a dishrag.

Jeanie's every muscle convulsed, and she was squeezed out, out into mid-air, her soul shooting like a star. Her arms and legs flew wide, and she landed on her back, with a little bounce. Her eyelids rolled closed.

◆

For the longest time, Jeanie couldn't open her eyes. She couldn't move. The smell of chemicals and burned plastic assaulted her. She lay there, listening to Sally wail. She heard Mr. Conti as well. They sounded distant, like the dogs had sounded before. She couldn't hear the dogs anymore.

The rain stopped as abruptly as it had started. The storm ended.

Jeanie felt herself lifted off the ground and carried, like a tiny baby. She couldn't tell who was carrying her, and her eyes still refused to open. Everything felt skewed. She felt smaller than normal, too lightweight. Her body seemed compact, as if maybe it weren't all there anymore.

Far-distant thunder rumbled, non-threatening.

"Crack o'doom," Jeanie thought. She couldn't speak.

Sally said, "My mom and dad are gonna be mad."

The walk took forever, or maybe Sally took his time. Jeanie didn't know. All she knew was that she was awake, but she couldn't open her eyes, and she couldn't speak. None of her muscles worked.

Sally's footsteps reached creaky stairs, then wood. A screen door slammed shut behind them. Sally climbed some stairs, opened a door and stepped through it. He sat Jeanie upon a cushion, upright, with something soft against her back.

One of Jeanie's eyes cracked open, halfway. The other felt stuck, crusty, wanting to roll upward, but unable. She saw that she was in a bedroom, but she could only stare straight ahead.

The eye was half open, but it didn't move in its socket.

In her peripheral vision, Jeanie saw the arms of the chair extending out on either side of her, larger than life, dwarfing her. She remembered that chair. She remembered it smaller.

Sally moved across Jeanie's field of vision. She watched him from beneath the one eyelid.

He paced in the narrow track between his bed and the wall. He undressed, stripping out of his wet clothes and throwing them on the floor. He dropped his underwear and left them where they fell.

Jeanie couldn't turn her head. She couldn't take her eye off the pallor of his skin, splotched red where he had pimples on his back and arms, on his bottom. His belly stuck out in front, and his hunched shoulders made him seem malformed.

It wasn't the first time Jeanie had seen him

without clothes. Memories of moonlit midnights, dancing under the full moon, the harvest moon, the blue moon, the wolf moon, the hunter's and the hay moon, with her parents, naked, and Sally's parents, naked, and Sally with his white skin that glowed in the moonlight, dancing and celebrating, good memories, filled Jeanie's head. The Contis had sung songs with words Jeanie didn't understand, and her parents had sung along. They had brought cakes and drinks that smelled like the garden and tasted sweet. On the solstice, Jeanie could stay up past her bedtime and eat as many of the special treats as she wanted. She could drink the magic juice to her heart's content. And she danced, naked, under the moon's watchful eye, with a cake in one hand and the world in the other, and her parents told her she was being groomed for greatness—because that's what the Contis told them.

Sally crossed to where Jeanie couldn't see him, but she heard him pull open a drawer. He tossed dry clothes onto the bed. They flashed into her line of sight and landed in the middle of the bedspread.

Raised voices, angry voices, came up the stairs—Mr. and Mrs. Conti. It was a brief storm, however, over almost as soon as it had begun.

Sally came back by the bed to dress. "My mom and dad are gonna be mad." Stepping into white briefs, he rushed and caught his foot in the leg-band.

He started to topple. He let go of the underpants and reached out to catch himself on the arm of Jeanie's chair. The chair shook, rattling Jeanie and tipping her to one side. Her one eye opened the rest of the way. The other rattled around in its socket, but the eyelid remained stuck shut.

Sally tugged up his underpants.

"Salvatore! Where are you?" Footsteps echoed in the stairwell outside the room.

Sally pulled on a pair of sweatpants. "My boy's in his room, Mom."

A small woman came into the room.

Mrs. Conti was tiny. Jeanie's dad had called her a little person. When the woman stood next to her son, she barely came above his belly.

"Are you okay?"

"Okay." Sally pulled a t-shirt on over his head.

"Are you hungry?"

He considered for a moment, then shook his head.

The woman took her son by the hand and led him to the bed. She jumped up to sit on it and patted it to indicate that he should sit, too.

Sally sat beside her, dipping the mattress low so that she slid up against him. "My mom and dad are gonna be mad."

"Why would we be mad?"

"The window is closing." Sally looked over at the chair. His mom followed his gaze and gasped softly.

For a long moment, no one said anything. Sally hung his head.

"I'm not mad. Salvatore, I'm not mad at you. Okay?"

"Okay."

"You did good. You showed your dad where Jeanie was."

Sally nodded.

The tiny woman folded her hands in her lap. "You remember what we said, right? Sometimes bad things happen to the people we love, and it's sad. But it's worth the sacrifice if it saves someone else. Do you understand?"

Sally nodded. He looked across at Jeanie and met her one-eyed gaze. "My boy will be normal."

Mrs. Conti rubbed up and down Sally's arm. "Yes, my darling boy. You'll be normal, and we'll move to a new place where no one knows us, and we'll start a new life there. It'll be wonderful. You'll see."

Sally's dad appeared in the doorway. He still wore his one-piece jumpsuit, torn at one thigh and stained at the knees. The brim of his hat dripped onto his shoulders, and the rest of him dripped onto the floor. He and Sally's mom exchanged a look. It was the look of grown-up secrets that Jeanie recognized well.

Mr. Conti nodded. "I've got her ready."

"Let's hope this works." Mrs. Conti slid off the bed and moved to the door. "At least, the rain'll wash away any evidence. You buried the gun deep?"

"Told you I did."

"Yeah, you told me you'd bring Jeanie straight home, too."

They made angry eyes at each other.

Mrs. Conti said, "I've got a bad feeling about this."

"Everything's going to be fine."

"'Any required change may be effected by the application of the proper kind... and degree... of Force...'"

Mr. Conti joined her, reciting the quotation from memory. "...in the proper manner, through the proper medium... to the proper object.' I know Crowley's damn postulate, woman."

"We had our object primed, and lightning's a pretty damn powerful Force."

Mr. Conti nodded, but not in a happy way, in a bad-day sort of way. "We don't know that it disrupted the magick."

"What if the lightning set her free? She could be anywhere. The only place we know for sure she isn't, is in the afterlife, 'cause we blocked her from that."

"It makes sense that she'd stay in her own body.

All we can do is perform the ritual and see what happens."

"Let's get it over with, then." The woman looked back at her son. "Come downstairs, Salvatore. It's ritual time."

"Okay." Sally rose. He paused to grab Jeanie, tucking her in the crook of one arm.

The world tipped askew for Jeanie. Her eye stared straight forward, locked open now, her only window on the world. When Sally turned, the dresser slid into Jeanie's view, and Jeanie saw Sally reflected in the mirror.

He stood there, with Dolly tucked in the crook of his arm. Half of Dolly's face had melted and blackened. Her hair was singed, her dungarees filthy. Jeanie saw a single blue, sparkle eye, staring back at her. The other was melted shut. All Jeanie could do was stare. She understood. Panic, like static electricity, crackled inside her and all over the immobile, plastic surface of her arms and legs.

Sally carried her out the bedroom door. He descended the stairs, and Jeanie caught glimpses of photos on the wall, pictures of Sally at all ages, from birth to adult. Most of the pictures showed him with his mom. As he got bigger and bigger, his mom looked smaller and smaller by comparison.

"Come in here, my boy."

Jeanie's insides crackled. She watched a living room go by and a hallway with a door that gave a peek into a bathroom. The kitchen came into view. It had white cabinets with shiny red handles and white linoleum on the floor.

"Come closer, Salvatore."

Sally moved deeper into the kitchen. The tabletop came into Jeanie's line of sight, and upon it, she saw a girl lying on her back, wet hair hanging off the edge of the table. Someone had removed the girl's clothes. Her chest and shoulders had bright red marks that looked like roots growing across them, under the skin. They branched and sent out shoots of scarlet tributaries that spread down her belly.

"I hope it's not too late."

"Get the boy in position. We're only going to get one shot at this."

Jeanie's line of sight shifted. She tried to close her eye, but the eyelid wouldn't budge, and all she could do was stare down into the girl's face. It had no life left in it. The girl's eyes were closed, but her mouth lay open, showing a blue-pink interior, tongue swollen and overflowing her bottom teeth. Jeanie recognized the face. It was her own.

"Don't be nervous, Salvatore," Mrs. Conti said. "This won't hurt a bit. Jeanie's going to be with you forever, inside, where she can help you be smarter.

You'll see. My boy will be normal. It'll be worth the sacrifice."

"Don't promise the boy something we're not sure we can produce."

"After all the trouble we went to, all the years of preparation, all those rituals to loosen her soul from its anchor and block it from the Light, I reckon some positive thinking couldn't hurt. Besides, if this doesn't work, it won't matter. We'll move on. We'll find another child and start all over again. And Salvatore, well, he'll never know the difference."

"I'll know," said Mr. Conti.

Sally's mom petted her son's arm absently, and her fingertips brushed the melted side of the doll's face. She jerked her hand away. "Salvatore, give me that filthy thing."

"Okay," Sally said.

Mrs. Conti took the doll from Sally, holding it by a heel.

Jeanie's world turned upside-down, and she saw Mr. Conti wrap his hand around a big, shiny knife.

Sally's mom opened a drawer and dropped the doll inside, into the old-fashioned trash compactor. She pushed down on the doll with the butt of her hand, compressing it into the paper, plastic and Styrofoam beneath it.

One blue, sparkle eye stared up through Mrs. Conti's fingers to Sally, who stood by the table. He reached out his big, man hand to stroke the other Jeanie's wet hair. Mr. Conti raised the knife in both hands, high over the other Jeanie's chest. He started to sing.

The compactor closed slowly, cutting off the light as it went, gradually, until Jeanie was left in complete darkness, giving her the welcome illusion that she had finally managed to close her eye. Inside the compactor, it was quiet. Mr. Conti's chanting sounded far away. Jeanie thought of her mom and dad. She thought of the dogs.

An engine rumbled to life.

"Do you have to do that now, woman?"

"Sorry. I wasn't thinking," said Sally's mom. "It's habit to turn it on when it's full."

"Well, too late now. Let it run. I'll start over when it's done."

"It'll only take a minute."

The trash compactor slowly squeezed its contents, making neat the discarded containers. When it crushed the doll's head, the hard plastic gave way with a loud *crack!*

"Crack o'doom," Sally said.

◆◆◆

# Coquettrice

The cockatrice clucked its tongue and sniffed at the steam rising off the eviscerated corpse. It narrowed its eyes with pleasure. Gently, it pushed its hands through the coils of intestine and the lumpy organs to savor the dissipating heat.

A sound at the end of the alley alerted the cockatrice to the intruder. It lifted its head and peered through the darkness with black-amber eyes. Those eyes tracked the man as he fronted a wall and opened his clothing to piss upon the brick. The cockatrice stood slowly, unfolding its long, lean body. It swayed there seductively. Its bare skin reflected what little luminescence lingered in the twilight of the man's life.

Even intoxicated, the man sensed something. In mid-stream, member in hand, he turned sharply toward the cockatrice. He looked confused, shocked even, and the cockatrice smiled. In a heartbeat, his last, the cockatrice struck.

◆

There was no warning, that morning, in the subtle shift of nebulae across the sky. I entered the bus, as usual, riding the same line to the same stop. The same dull faces shared my commute. The same inane conversations grumbled at the periphery of my consciousness.

And then, "Hi," she said, "Mind if I sit here?" It was such a simple opening to such a complex story. At the time, I didn't hear the weight in her request. Remembering back, I don't see how I could have missed it. Her smile alone, so sweet, should have made me wary.

I looked her over: high breasts, flat stomach, jeans tight enough to camel-toe in her fleshy crotch, long legs, pretty face and that smile.

Momentarily, "Sure," I replied and moved my books off the seat, holding them in my lap with the spines facing her so she could see the titles.

She looked.

"Oh. You're a doctor?" They all asked that once they'd seen the clues and always with that same feminine squeak of interest in their voices.

I gave my customary chuckle and response, "Soon. I start my internship this fall." Offer the hand. Smile. "Name's William. What's yours?" Tip the head with interest and look straight into the eyes. My choreography worked every time.

"Tiffani." She turned toward me and slid her hand into mine. I noticed how soft it was, how frail and light. The kind of hand a man loves to have stroking him.

I got her phone number and called her after my last class. I asked her out. She agreed. Readily. Dinner and a walk along the river led us back to my place.

I rubbed my fingertips in lazy circles at the base of her spine, naked with her upon the stain of our union. Her hand languidly coaxed me up from the languor into which I had drifted.

"What are you doing?" I asked dreamily.

"Playing."

"Playing? Are you having fun?"

"Oh, yes."

"Good. Me too."

"Good."

I realized that this was a woman I could love.

◆

The German shepherd growled and bared its teeth, so the cockatrice twisted its head off. Afterward, the monster looked up at the house, holding the decapitation by an ear. Blood and other fluids drained from the dog's neck onto the lawn. Stepping over the twitching body, the cockatrice rounded the corner of the house and peered through a window. It purred deep in its throat at what it saw. It cut through the screen with one, sharp claw and crawled inside. Television noise came from another room. The cockatrice quietly shut the nursery door. It walked to the crib and held up the dog's head for approval, bobbing it above the railing like a puppet with a ribbon tongue and blank, button eyes. The child giggled. For several minutes, the cockatrice amused itself, making the baby laugh. Predatory peek-a-boo pleased it for awhile, but not forever. The sour-sweet aroma of infant-meat made its mouth water.

◆

An idyllic summer, spent in the arms of my sunny-tressed Tiffani, turned into a cruel autumn. The leaves gathered age-spots; they cringed, dried up and died. Tiffani and I moved in together. I started my internship and began my decline.

Indian summer they called it, but that only brought images of hatchets and scalpings—blond hair clutched in my fist. She wasn't home when I returned. It wasn't the first time. Tiffani said she got bored while I was on duty. She went out with *friends*.

At first, I believed her. I waited with a book, pretending to read between glances at the clock, the door, the window. My mind buzzed with questions that grew more and more urgent, more and more bitter with each passing minute. Finally, the key turned in the lock, and I was up and at the bedroom doorway in a second. I watched her sneak into the darkened apartment and saw her surprise as she caught my eyes upon her.

"Hi, William," she said with that smile.

"Where have you been?" I accused.

"Out."

"Out where? Who were you with?"

"Shopping, silly." Tiffani set her packages aside and slithered up to me. She pressed her cold hands against my cheeks. Her lips grazed mine, and her tongue flickered to taste me.

My gut sensed another man, but I wanted desperately to believe her. I kissed her deeply, searching for hope. That night, we made love like never before. I had something to prove: my manhood, my love, my ownership. I proudly chained her to me with three solid orgasms. Foolish as I was, I thought that would be enough, enough to keep her satisfied and tied to my bed.

The pretenses helped for a while. Tiffani and I discussed the weather. We made love. We did our weekly shopping. We curled up on the couch to watch movies. We kissed hello and good-bye. We ate, and we slept, but time and again, I came home to an empty apartment. I found bus tickets to odd parts of town. I smelled cigarettes on her clothes and in her hair, and I overheard quickly-ended phone conversations, "No. Don't worry. He doesn't suspect a thing. I have to go."

On a Sunday, a strange woman came to the door saying her name was Debora and claiming to be a friend of Tiffani's. I let her in. Tiffani was dressing in the bedroom.

"So," Debora said with a conspiratorial wink, "you're the cock?"

"What?"

Debora looked past my shoulder, her face suddenly pinched with guilty secrets. I looked too.

Tiffani stood there. I caught the tail-end of her head shaking, her eyes hard with warning, then she showered me with one of her pearlescent smiles.

I left them to their lame excuses and isolated myself in the bedroom. The cock. The Cock. That's what they called him. My beautiful Tiffani was screwing the Cock. The crudeness of it turned my stomach.

Over the next couple weeks, I noticed dark clouds gathering under my eyes. I lost my appetite for food. My clothes irritated me, and finally, my libido left me. Tiffani swore it didn't matter, but I could feel the chains weakening.

My suspicions haunted me. The hallways of

the hospital echoed with her name. Thoughts of her breezy, frail hands stalked me as I inserted catheters. Images of her thighs, spread wide, plagued me as I drove needles through the walls of veins. I saw her mouth open and willing as I threaded tubes down throats. The specters of her sexuality, however, had lost their eroticism. They bedded in betrayal.

October was coming to an end, burying the corpse of autumn in the grave of winter. Anyone who ever said winter didn't start until December had never lived in Minneapolis. The season cheated there. It snuck in early. It double-dealt doubt and dread throughout the city long before its victims admitted that it had arrived.

I remember the date: October 29. Tiffani wasn't home when I got off work. I pretended to read until midnight. From midnight to two, I paced. By two-thirty, I was cursing her and the Cock, raging and swearing. By four, I was in bed. She came home, and I pretended to be asleep.

With dawn came a new understanding of what I had to do. I climbed carefully out of bed. I showered, shaved and brushed my teeth. I dressed in my usual work clothes. I left the apartment at the usual time and walked to the usual bus stop. I got on the usual bus.

I got off again at the very next stop and sneaked back to spy.

Despite everything, despite her lies, and despite her slip-ups, a part of me still wanted to believe her. That hope-filled morsel stirred up enough doubt that I *had* to find out for sure. I couldn't just leave her. I'd wonder for the rest of my life whether I'd been wrong. Maybe she really had been telling the truth. Maybe 'the Cock' *was* just her pet name for me, as unflattering as it was. Maybe. Maybe. Maybe. Too many maybes.

For two long hours I stood on the street, in the cold, waiting for Tiffani to leave the apartment. Following her was a lot easier than I'd expected. She didn't take a bus or a taxi. Her destination was a three-story brownstone only five blocks from where we lived. The front door of the building opened with a squeak as I followed her inside. It startled me. Guilt stirred in my brainstem, but I was beyond listening to my feeble conscience.

Tiffani's footsteps echoed in the staircase that spiraled squarely overhead. I could just make out the edge of her coat as she ascended. She was on the second floor, turning to climb to the third. Her slim hand wrapped delicately over the railing, gliding along as she went.

I tracked her with my eyes to the third floor. She knocked. I could tell the sound came from the rear of the building, but I couldn't tell which apartment.

Cautiously, I climbed halfway to the second story, peering upward, and heard a door open on the third. I froze.

"Hi," Tiffani said. Simple, straightforward: that was her way.

I strained my ears but heard no response aside from the eventual closing of the door and the slide of a deadbolt. I don't know how long I stood there on the landing between the first and second floor. My heart raced, and my head pounded. I considered leaving, forgetting the whole thing, but I couldn't. My need to know rooted me. I stared at the wall's chipped plaster and flaking paint. I imagined Tiffani upstairs in some other man's arms. Before I could change my mind, I climbed the rest of the stairs.

The light fixture on the third floor cast a jaundiced glow. Two apartments sheltered at the back of the building, numbers 11 and 12. One was fronted by a flowered mat. I discounted that one and turned to inspect the other. A Halloween decoration hung on the door, but not the usual cutesy witch or jangling skeleton. An oil painting, approximately five by seven inches, it flaunted the kind of imagination I would never possess and triggered a sort of morbid fascination that escalated as I studied it. A taxidermied snake framed the painting. The creature's markings were a subtle pattern of brown and black diamonds.

Its skin flaked in places and its tail tucked neatly into its mouth at the top.

Upon the canvas, the artist had rendered the profile of a rooster, just the head. Its feathers were a bruised black-and-blue, iridescent. Its comb was swollen and ruddy; its visible eye was dark and dirty amber with a circular iris. As I examined it, I realized that the rooster's beak purposely resembled a penis, erect with a natural, downward curve. Its wattle hung below like wrinkled, scarlet testicles. The image disgusted me. Whoever this guy was, he was sick.

This guy was the Cock. The connection fired in my brain like a flare and left behind the acrid taste of fury. Of course.

I glared at the painting.

The rooster stared back at me, unblinking.

Tiffani's laughter whispered out to me—yes, she was in there. I raised my fist to knock, but hesitated. The hackles at the back of my neck tickled and gave me a violent shiver. I tried to rub the feeling away.

The rooster stared at me.

Suddenly, I lost the courage to go on. I realized abruptly that if I knocked it would end my relationship with Tiffani, whether she was guilty or not. Defeated, I turned to leave.

A man stood at the top of the stairs behind me. I hadn't heard him approach. He wore all black: trench coat, shirt and twilled-cotton trousers. His head was ragged and scruffy, despite the clean lines of his body and the penetrating sharpness of his ice-blue eyes. I waved my hand negligently at the painting and muttered some pseudo-excuse for loitering in the hall, then tried to hurry past him. He stopped me with a hand on my arm. I bristled.

"Beware the Basilisk," he uttered, his voice full of apocalyptic melodrama. He nodded toward number 12.

"What?" I was flustered. The man stood several inches taller than me and was built for a boxing ring. Something about him regressed me into a child caught in a misdemeanor.

The man scrutinized my guilt. He said nothing more, but withdrew a flyer from his pocket and thrust it into my hand.

I watched him walk to number 11, unlock the door, wipe his feet on the flowered mat and disappear inside. I shoved the brochure into my coat pocket and hurried back down the stairs. In the foyer, I paused only long enough to read the name on mailbox number 12: 'P.J. Price'. I repeated it to myself, several times, and then I rushed out the front door. The cold air hit my cheeks like water on embers.

◆

Through the peephole at apartment number 11, Father Matthew watched the young intern flee. Previously, he had only seen William in pictures taken by a local priest to document the coven and the people connected to it. Immediately, Father Matthew had recognized William's innocence. How could he have missed the brush strokes of embarrassment upon William's cheeks and the pain in his eyes?

Humming a simple hymn, Matthew crossed his meagerly furnished apartment and hung his coat in the closet. He made tea and plain toast for dinner, gave a short prayer of thanks for the meal, then ate in silence. When finished, he pushed aside his plate and settled in to study. First, he picked up the file on the intern, William Jason Leake. It included the young man's birth certificate, baptism certificate, I.Q. test scores, grade school report, high school transcript, university transcript, credit report, residential history, medical records, gun license, psychological evaluation, and finally, the report on William's habits and internship. Matthew had already memorized nearly everything in it, but he knew the value of thoroughness. Browsing through the pages, Matthew wished he could do more to help William, but he had more to worry about than a young man who was going to walk away with only a broken heart.

The priest knew William was in no danger. The

historical profile indicated that Tiffani Cerastes had probably chosen William as her cover. She lived with him to preserve an illusion of normalcy. His mundanity helped her disassociate herself from her crimes. Matthew figured Tiffani would dump William shortly before the ritual and move in with the Cock to raise the newborn cockatrice.

Matthew looked over at his rooster. It stirred, scratching its feet in the sandy floor of its cage. Matthew tossed it a piece of left-over crust from his toast and watched as the animal eyed the offering. The rooster didn't wait long before snatching up the bread. It ate with a ruffle of red-orange feathers. Matthew turned back to the table. He closed William's file and set it aside. Then, he picked up his Bible and opened it to "Psalms."

The light coming in the window turned from golden twilight to cold streetlight, and Matthew read aloud the words that most comforted him, "Thou shalt not be afraid for the terror by night; nor for the arrow that flieth by day; nor for the pestilence that walketh in darkness; nor for the destruction that wasteth at noonday. A thousand shall fall at thy side...." So many had died at Matthew's side. So many had given their lives in the Holy War that all mortal wars emulated. He knew that someday he too would die in the Lord's service.

"...And ten thousand at thy right hand." Matthew had killed in the name of the Lord. He had lost count, long ago, of the minions he had sent to Hell. Sometimes innocents got in the way, and that may have been a shame, but it was also a necessary price to pay.

"...But it shall not come nigh thee."

Taking a deep breath, Matthew closed the Good Book and said a short, silent prayer, finishing aloud with, "Lord, give me strength and wisdom to overcome Basilisk and his cockatrice. Amen."

◆

In the candlelit room, the orgiastic pile of bodies writhed. The cockatrice had one in its mouth and one in its sex. It moaned its pleasure and lifted its eyes to gaze up the body of its future husband. When in its true form, as it was then, the change in its eyes gave everything a fire-shimmer, as if it were looking through an amber lens. It preferred this demon's form to the soft, weak femininity it hid in most of the time, but it had too many enemies to show its unvarnished visage to the mortal world.

The cockatrice sucked and licked as its lover ejaculated into its throat. So succulent, he was. His musky-sweet seed tantalized the cockatrice's blood-lust. The taste thrilled the monster, but it wasn't beast enough to kill this one. No, this one had a purpose. The cockatrice growled as its own orgasm rippled through its body.

◆

Back at home, I tossed my coat aside and paced, waiting. I barely noticed the shadows shifting across my apartment as night's darkness menaced the day away. All I could see was that genital-faced rooster and my Tiffani. In my mind, it pecked at her, and she laughed. She laughed again and again. Eventually, she was laughing at me, and then he joined her, crowing at the gullible boyfriend. I cursed them both, and I cursed my own stupidity. I was ready for her when she finally came in the door. By then, I had settled onto the couch like a crucified saint, ankles crossed and arms spread along its back. That's how I felt, me and my martyrdom.

I hadn't bothered to turn on any lights and I took some satisfaction in her startlement when I spoke to her out of the darkness, "Get enough?"

"Jesus, William. You scared me." She turned on the lights and must have seen the accusation in my face, or perhaps in my eyes. She did a double-take, then began to explain without having to be asked,

"Debora and I went shopping."

"Where's your bags?"

"I beg your pardon?"

"Your bags. You went shopping, but you didn't buy anything?" I liked the taste of self-righteousness.

"Oh. I must have left them at Debora's place. We stopped there afterward for coffee."

"Does Debora live in a three-story brownstone?"

Tiffani muttered something unintelligible and walked into the bedroom. I arose and followed. She had thrown her coat on the bed and was sitting beside it, removing a boot. I leaned against the doorjamb.

"Excuse me?" I said, cool as a snake, "I didn't hear what you said."

"I said yes, she does." Tiffani paused, then asked, "How do you know that?"

I ignored her question. I had to ask, despite or maybe because of the cliché, "Was he good?"

"What? Who?"

"The guy in number 12. The Cock." My mouth opened obscenely around the last word.

"You followed me?"

I responded with a crooked, drunken grin, even though I hadn't had a drop of alcohol. It fit.

"How dare you follow me!"

I used my doctor voice, the one she hated, logical and cold. "How dare you screw around on me."

"I'm not."

"No? Then who's P.J.? Who's the Cock?" I was beginning to like the vindictive, violent feeling that word had in my mouth.

"P.J.?"

"Yeah. P.J. Price. You know. The one you're screwing?"

"P.J.? Oh. You mean Paul. He's just a friend. I'm not sleeping with him!"

I should have expected it. How could I argue with that? I hadn't *seen* her in bed with the guy. I'd only seen her go inside and heard her laugh. She had blown my case right out of the water. She knew it too. She came over to reinforce her words with kisses and caresses. It was my word against hers, and all I had was jealousy and conjecture in my corner.

My confidence was abandoning me, but I made one last feeble attempt to rally my side, "Then why did you lie and tell me you went shopping with Debora?"

"Because," she pouted, "you're so jealous. I didn't think you'd understand if I said I'd spent the afternoon hanging out with a male friend. I'm sorry, honey."

A man knows when a woman has him by the balls.

◆

The morning sun cast a flaccid light down upon Father Matthew. He stood on the street across from William and Tiffani's apartment building, rocking on his heels. He buried his hands in his pockets and tried to ignore the cold's saturation into his bones. He watched. Heaven only knew what he expected to see or what great influence he hoped to have by being there, but some divine hint of instinct had sent him.

Eventually, the young intern emerged from the building. Matthew noted William looked tired and tense. Innocent, the priest thought. Innocent enough that he sensed the truth about his lover only on a subconscious level.

Their eyes met. Matthew stood firm, knowing that William had seen him. He gave the young man his most intense stare. 'Listen to your gut, boy,' the look sent. 'Run. Run away as fast and as far as you can. Go. Go. Go.' A city bus drove slowly past. Matthew watched as William ran to catch it.

◆

The hospital buzzed, coughed, gurgled, cried, and blip-blip-blipped. I hated it. I intended to go into private practice where I could diagnose my patients, then refer them to a hospital or specialist for treatment. I liked solving puzzles but hated doing

the hands-on dirty-work. I had learned two important lessons as an intern: one, that the textbooks did
a thoroughly cosmetic cover-up on the truth of human anatomy—bodies were actually disgusting, filthy
things that oozed, stank, and housed parasites—and
two, that people were unbelievably stupid. They all
thought they were invulnerable, that they could stick
anything they wanted in any orifice, play with dy-
namite, or leap tall buildings in a single bound, and
walk away intact. They were usually wrong.

My dinner break came at seven p.m., and I took
it promptly. Getting through the line at the cafete-
ria chewed up fifteen minutes; eating took another
fifteen. To pass the rest of the time, I found a quiet
phone cubicle and called home. It rang through, and
I muttered to Tiffani to pick up. She didn't. I hung
up and redialed only to reach more emptiness. The
hollow rings sounded like sonar pings searching for
something solid off which to bounce, but they found
only a growing void. I began to feel sick.

◆

Father Matthew saw her through his peephole.
Tiffani Cerastes knocked on the door across the hall.
Her delicate fingers brushed over the beak of the
painted rooster. Matthew admired her beauty, as

any man would. He had taken a vow of celibacy and dedicated his life to a higher purpose, but that didn't mean he couldn't feel the stirring in his loins at the sight of an attractive woman, especially a cockatrice. He briefly touched himself through his pants, drawing strength from the physical energy that fired at the sensation.

The door opened at number 12. Paul Jefferson Price stood there dressed only in a pair of blue jeans. His upper torso rippled with muscles—smooth, full and strong. The young man was handsome, of course. Basilisk would have it no other way. Matthew waited until Tiffany had entered, and the door had shut behind her, then he went back to the kitchen table.

The clock struck eight, with soft, reminder chimes. Matthew picked up his notebook, opened it to a new page and began to write in his economical, masculine script:

*8 p.m. Tiffani Cerastes arrives at no. 12 and enters. Price inside. I no longer have any doubt that Cerastes is the Mother for the unholy birthing. She now wears Basilisk's mark upon her left hand. I saw it only moments ago while she waited for the Cock to let her inside the coven room. She will guide the ritual and tend to the Cock. Once the egg has hatched, assuming I fail in my attempt to stop the entire process, she will mother the infant cockatrice to maturity.*

*The ward remains on the door, making it impossible to enter, even when the apartment is empty. They're careful. So much is at stake. Tonight, Basilisk will manifest, and once he is in this world I can banish him back to Hell. I pray for the innocent and ask that the Lord....*

A knock on the door drew Matthew from his journal. He closed it, stood and crossed the room. Peering through the peephole, he spied a little devil with baby horns, rosy cheeks, and a pointed tail that bounced on its own. He unlocked and opened the door.

"Trick or treat!" the children cried in relative unison, holding up their bags.

Matthew smiled and reached for his plastic pumpkin of candy.

◆

I called the apartment every fifteen minutes after that first time. My agitation grew with each unanswered ring. Finally, I made the hospital let me go home. My stomach had knotted up a half an hour earlier. I knew what I had to do.

The 8:30 bus arrived five minutes late. I pushed through the waiting commuters to get to it, my pardons growing more urgent and less polite as the bus's doors slowly closed without me.

"Wait!" I called, stepping up and pounding on the glass. The driver reopened the doors. I climbed in, paid my fare, found a seat near the middle and stared out the bus window. My hands clenched into fists over and over on my thighs, until I felt eyes upon me. I looked over to see a woman watching me. I caught her gaze, and she turned away. Irritated, I shifted my posture toward the window and stuffed my hands in my pockets. My fingers brushed the flyer. I thought of the strange man who had given it to me and remembered seeing him outside my apartment that morning. I pulled it out and looked at it.

"Judas walks among us," it said, superimposed over a dull reproduction of 'The Last Supper,' and I almost threw it away right then and there. I had little interest in sanctimonious propaganda. I opened it, however, curious about the man himself.

Even as upset as I was, the interior text made me laugh, albeit wryly. It talked about demons and their servants. In particular, it mentioned Basilisk, the Snake King, who impregnated roosters that then laid eggs out their bowels. From these eggs, the cockatrice hatched. According to the flyer, the cockatrice were monsters that served Basilisk and could change form to become beautiful women. They "seduced innocent men into sin." The brochure went on to explain how they killed for fun, ate human flesh and had uncanny powers, including the ability to mesmerize their victims. I tossed the flyer on the floor of the bus.

When I got home, the apartment was dark.

"Tiff?" I called, on the one small hope that she had fallen asleep. No answer. No *fucking* answer. She wasn't there. I knew what *was* there though: my gun.

◆

Father Matthew's evening dragged. He busied himself with scripture and prayer. He double-blessed his primary weapon: the rooster whose crow could return Basilisk to Hell. He also prepared his other weapon. The revolver felt good in his hand as he cleaned and then reloaded it.

Matthew had finished his last journal entry a few minutes earlier at 9 p.m. In it, he had documented the arrival of the other coven members, four of them, two men and two women. Finally, he had gathered up all his files and placed them, with the journal, in the Little Black Box. The clergy would look for that if anything happened to him. He locked the box and duct-taped it to the inner frame of the couch. As he replaced the piece of furniture, his scalp crawled and itched. He scratched it, turning slowly to stare at the locked door. The unholy rituals had begun across the hall. The rooster felt it too. It fretted, ruffling its feathers uneasily.

The priest sat at the table and prayed over his rosary, "Though I walk through the valley of the shadow of death...." A sharp pain lit up his calf. Matthew cringed and drew his leg up protectively. He raised his pant-leg and examined the source of the pain. Two puncture wounds sat side-by-side on his calf, already swelling and bleeding. Looking down to the floor, Matthew spotted his attacker.

The snake wasn't large, only about two feet long and meaty. It looked like braided leather, its markings a series of diamonds all fit neatly together. The beast lifted its ovoid head and swayed. It delivered its second strike to the priest's other ankle, sinking fangs deep into Matthew's flesh.

Matthew threw himself to the floor, toppling the chair toward the snake in an attempt to escape another bite.

The viper struck again.

Matthew grabbed the chair with both hands. He beat the creature. Chair-legs splintered and the sound of cracking wood filled the apartment. With desperate satisfaction, he saw portions of the snake's body split and smear, flatten and bleed. He hit it again and again. His arms and back ached with the effort, but Matthew didn't stop until the snake ceased moving.

The animal died as it had arrived: silently.

Matthew dragged himself toward the counter. He reached up to pull himself to his feet and his gaze landed on the rooster. It lay wrong, one foot twitching. Matthew's legs denied him, and he slumped back to the floor. He easily imagined, if not actually felt, the venom coursing through his blood stream.

"Help!" he shouted, trying to reach anyone. "Help!" He called again and again. Eventually, he whimpered his pleas, "Oh... Lord... oh please, God...." A heavy, black shroud enfolded Matthew. His eyes froze in place, unblinking, and his throat constricted on the prayer, unheard. He had failed.

◆

I climbed the stairs to the third floor of the brownstone. The gun felt heavy in my coat pocket; its solid presence bumped against my thigh with each step. I had lost all feeling and all reason. Draped in a veil of sanguine rage, I stood at the door to number 12. Someone had removed the rooster painting.

Without hesitation, I reached for the doorknob and turned it. I swung the door wide and stepped across the threshold. A giant bed stood in the middle of the room, draped with red and black, sheeted with satin. Candles cast a carnal glow. Two faces looked over at me. His, so handsome, so smug, had a smile. Hers, so beautiful, so familiar, showed surprise. They were naked. He rolled over and sat up. I saw his erection.

"William?" she murmured, moving to the edge of the bed. "What are you...?"

I pulled my gun.

"William!"

I didn't think. I just pulled the trigger. The explosion rebounded off my nerves and hit the wall. My finger twitched again. The second bullet threw the Cock back onto the pillows. He was bleeding. His blood drained slowly, creating a scarlet river that meandered down his heaving chest to pool in the basin of his stomach. He hissed, deflated and died.

Someone closed the door behind me, and I felt two people, one on either side, take my arms, take my gun, and take my freedom. I didn't struggle. It was too late for that.

"What do we do now?" The others whispered among themselves. "The Cock is dead. We're doomed."

I began to shake.

Tiffani stood. She smiled that smile and tilted her head just so, "William. Will you never cease to surprise me?" She crossed toward me, her breasts swaying with each step. Dribbles of splattered blood,

P.J.'s blood, ran down her hip. Her eyes looked strange. The whites slowly darkened to black crystal sparked with amber. Her pupils became discs of obsidian. As she approached, she changed. Like some walking special-effect, she transformed before my eyes into a snake woman with talons and rippling muscles where feminine curves had once made her so shapely. Her skin took on a snake-like texture, and her body swallowed her hair leaving her completely bald. The bones in her face elongated and her mouth widened into a slash with the hint of a cleft lip. When her tongue flickered out, it had a forked tip. I stared, trying to see through the hallucination to the Tiffani I knew, but she eluded me. Hot urine ran down my legs and soaked into my shoes.

Tiffani announced, "We have a new Cock. Basilisk has sent us a sign." She touched her slim, cool fingers to my cheek. Her gaze mesmerized me. I relaxed.

Time and reality slipped away. They stripped me, the five of them. The two men held me in place while the three women bathed me thoroughly. Tiffani's friend Debora was there, but I had never seen the others. They bent me over an armchair. The enema made me uncomfortable. I cried. I begged.

I shat soup into an iron bucket.

Tiffani soothed me with tender caresses, as she always had. She assured me everything would be all right. She told me that Basilisk had chosen me. She stroked my penis with her frail, soft hand.

They tied my wrists to my ankles and placed me on the bed with my ass in the air. I turned my head to avoid looking at P.J. Price's gaping eyes and mouth. My cheek lay upon soft satin. Tiffani rubbed me with sharp-scented oils, massaging away my tension and fears. This *was* my Tiffani, after all. She wouldn't let anyone hurt me. She loved me. I closed my eyes. Her hands spread the oils over my skin and into my pores. She lubricated my anus with it, inside and out.

At some point, the chanting began. Deep and throaty, the lullaby made me sleepier. It wrapped me with a blanket of security. I even forgot that the underside of my naked body was exposed to the room. I wanted to forget everything.

"Soon, darling," Tiffani hissed into my ear. "It will all be over soon, and then we can go home." She blindfolded me, and I welcomed the darkness. No one could look at Basilisk and survive, she explained.

Their voices rose. I smelled burning hair and sulfur. I tracked their softly padding steps as they danced around the room. I was losing sensation in my hands and feet. I made fists and curled my toes to pass the time. Cool air fanned across my buttocks. The chanting grew louder, ecstatic and more insistent. The air itself crackled with energy, and the hair on the back of my neck stood on end. Someone touched me, and I instinctually tried to look behind myself. The blindfold denied me.

They were hands—large, masculine hands. They rubbed harshly over the fleshy hemispheres of my ass, kneading and spreading them. Something insinuated itself inside me. It was thin, limp and alive like a snake. Panic enveloped me, and my heart thundered. I cried out for Tiffani, for mercy and for God. I squirmed, but those hot hands held me firmly in place. The tentacle wiggled inside me, delving deeper and deeper. It swelled, filling me and spreading me wide. I screamed, I'm sure of it.

I thought my intestines would rupture from the sheer girth of it. It pulsed with a seductive new rhythm, with an alien heartbeat that tried to derail my own. The pain was excruciating.

Suddenly, the hands viced down on my hips. Basilisk raped me with a hard, heavy beat. He grunted with each thrust, then abruptly, the expanding tentacle erupted. It released its load of molten semen into my body. I heard Basilisk's unearthly groan as the demon came inside me, and I felt hopeful relief thread through my soul. Soon, the pain would end. The tentacle slithered out of me and went away. Basilisk loosened his hold on my hips, and I swear I felt him caress me, tenderly, just like my Tiffani had done. My screams subsided into sobs. I think I lost consciousness.

When I awoke, my anus hurt. Sticky with drying semen and blood, it burned. I couldn't move. My testicles descended from their clutch of fear and horror, to hang between the A-frame of my thighs. My knees ached. The sheet was hot beneath my cheek, wet with my own spit and rank with the perfume of anointing oils. The skin of my face tightened with dried brine and my throat felt as if I'd swallowed a handful of thistles.

They gathered around me; their master had retreated to his unholy realm. I felt their kisses, their caresses and their licking tongues as they cleaned me and adored me. They plugged me up, to keep the precious seed from escaping. Tiffani untied me, pulled away the blindfold and smiled into my eyes. She loved me.

The next couple days passed in a blur. The others took P.J. away and put new sheets on the bed. Tiffani stayed with me. We slept, ate and held each other, always naked. Tiffani insisted on doing everything for me. She fed me, spooning an herbal pudding into my mouth, and held the cup as I drank honeyed tea. She washed me and combed my hair. I began to feel like a king.

The egg formed slowly, soft and tender at first. The pressure coalesced into one place, like beads of mercury all rolling together to form one big, shimmery pool. Tiffani explained it all to me. I was going to be a father.

On the morning of the third day, the egg was a solid presence in my body. The thought of excreting it frightened me, but Tiffani assured me that everything would be fine. She was right. The egg came that evening. I squatted upon the bed, tears streaming down my cheeks, my groans and screams echoing in my head. It stretched me. It tore me. I thought for sure I would die, but finally, it was out. The egg was large, the size of a man's fist, enough to hold a supernaturally tiny infant. The shell gleamed with black and blue opalescence. The others cleaned it off while I lay gasping on the bed.

Later, Tiffani and I curled around it, keeping it warm between our bodies. I petted its dappled surface with awe-struck fingers. My baby grew inside it. For two weeks, Tiffani and I took turns leaving the bed to stretch, wash and use the bathroom. Most of the time, we cuddled, stroked each other, and made love with our baby lying beside us. The bed became our love nest.

On November 13 at 7:53 a.m., the egg cracked. Tiffani and I cried together as our child stretched a perfect, little arm out of her shell. We helped her emerge and cleaned away the thick, clear fluid in which she had incubated. She was beautiful and healthy. I loved her immediately. We had already chosen her name, Coquette. In French, Coquette meant 'flirtatious.' Lying there with my new family, I held Coquette's hand carefully in mine and kissed the delicate, baby fingers with their tiny talons and cool skin. She looked up at me, beguilingly, with her mother's black-amber eyes. I vowed to give her the world.

# Ardie Sue

Ardenia Sue Johnson was a black girl who had spent all eighteen of her years in Money, Mississippi, running barefoot on the banks of the Tallahatchie River. In all that time, she'd never wished to live anywhere else—not until that night.

Ardenia rocked on the porch swing. In her hand, she held a piece of paper folded over and over until it was as tiny as she could make it. The note fit squarely in the palm of her hand. She had its message memorized. It said simply, "I can't wait to see you again. Justin."

The sun was low in the western sky. As its heat dissipated, it left a breeze in its wake. The breeze sifted through the tired branches of the old willow and made the leaves of Grandma Johnson's dogwood shiver.

Ardenia's father sat on the couch in the living room, watching television. He looked over his shoulder and out the front window to the porch.

"Ardie Sue, get in here, please, and set the table for your mama!"

"Yes, Daddy." But Ardie didn't get up. She rocked back on the bench swing, planted her feet on the painted floor and extended her legs to their most graceful length. She bent over and looked at her shins. She wasn't allowed to shave them. Her mother said that only white girls shaved, that black women were proud of their bodies as God gave them. But other black girls in her high school shaved.

Ardie lifted her feet and freed the swing. She let it carry her back and forth with her legs stuck straight out in front of her. Gradually, it lost momentum. She got up and entered the house through the weathered, screen door. It slammed behind her.

Her father looked up from the couch. "What've I told you about slamming that door, girl?" He didn't wait for an answer but turned back to the television. He dug his large, spidery hand in a bowl of peanut husks on his lap, searching—without looking—for one that hadn't already been cracked.

Ardie leaned against the doorjamb to the living room and stashed the note from Justin in her pocket.

On the television, Walter Cronkite sat in his sky-blue suit in front of a backdrop showing the Apollo 14 lunar module. His mustache jumped. "...asked whether Astronaut Alan Shepherd has been out golfing since he got back on Planet Earth."

Ardie would have sworn she saw his eyes twinkle.

"If he has," Ardie's father told the anchor man, "I hope his aim's better'n Spiro Agnew's." He laughed at his own joke, though Ardie didn't get it.

Ardie's sister, Sissy, was lying on the floor watching the television. She rolled over and said, "Daddy, tell us the story about Bijou and the lynch mob."

Ardie's father looked over in surprise. "Why you want to hear that old ghost story?"

Sissy shrugged, and her gaze turned to Ardie.

The image behind Mr. Cronkite switched to Richard Nixon, and Ardie shoved off the doorjamb.

Ardie's father shook his head. "Ghost stories are for night-time, Missy Sissie. Let's see how we feel tonight, before bed. Okay?"

"Okay."

Ardie's mother was in the kitchen, stirring greens in a blackened, iron skillet. Sweat glimmered on her brow, and a few corkscrew curls had escaped from her braid like springs from a broken cuckoo clock. When she cooked, her wide bottom moved in counterpoint to the swish of her arm.

"Your daddy send you in here?" She looked Ardie over, top to toes, her dark eyes evaluating.

"Yes, Mama. To set the table." The smell of heated bacon grease made Ardie's mouth water.

"Good. The napkins are in the laundry basket. They're clean."

Ardie retrieved and folded the four cloth napkins her mother had made. She set out plates, glasses, and utensils on the kitchen table.

"I heard you got a boyfriend." Her mother opened the refrigerator and bent to look in it.

"No."

"I heard you been seen walking with that Laconi boy." She emerged with a jar of relish.

"He's just a friend." Ardie's face flushed. She moved the salt and pepper from the stove to the table. "That's all."

"That's all?"

"Yes, ma'am." Ardie busied her hands and eyes, adjusting utensils.

"You got to be careful, Ardie."

"I know, Mama."

"Things are different here from the rest of the world. You can't behave like what you see on the television."

"I know, Mama."

"You got to respect the old ways, or...."

"I *know*, Mama. You don't have to worry. He's not my boyfriend." Ardie met her mother's gaze, but only for a moment.

"All right," her mother said. "Call your daddy and Sissy in for supper."

◆

After supper, Ardie and Sissy settled into the bedroom they shared. Sissy sat on the floor, reading. She had their father's slim build, whereas Ardie took after their more compact mother.

Ardie lay on her bed, on her belly, surrounded by schoolbooks. She looked up to find Sissy's eyes on her. "What?"

"Nothin'," said Sissy. "Just wonderin'."

"What?"

"I dunno."

"What, Sissy? Spit it out. I got work to do."

"You like Justin Laconi?"

Ardie looked toward the door. "Maybe."

"I wish you didn't."

"Hush. Keep your voice down. Ain't none of your business."

"I'm worried, Ardie Sue."

"There's nothing to worry about."

"What about the lynch mob?"

Ardie sighed. "Girl, that's just an old story they tell children to scare 'em. You're not a baby anymore."

"It ain't just a story."

"Yes. It is. There isn't any lynch mob. This is 1971, for Heaven's sake."

Sissy crossed her arms on her chest. "So?"

"So, there's no such thing as ghosts."

"I'd just rather you stayed away from him. What do you see in him anyway?"

"He's nice. Okay? He's just real nice."

Sissy shook her head. "I got a bad feeling in my gut, like somethin's stirrin'."

"The only thing stirrin' in there is your supper."

An hour later, they abandoned their studies and joined their parents in the living room.

"You got here in the nick-a-time, girl," her father said. "Andy Williams is about to come on."

Ardie stopped in her tracks. "What? No." Her hands fluttered. "We can't watch Andy Williams. *Mission: Impossible* is on tonight. I been waitin' all week for this, Daddy."

When Ardie's father laughed, it filled the entire room, rippled through the house and out into the yard. "I'm pulling your leg, girl."

Ardie rolled her eyes. She took a seat in the armchair. Her father was on the couch, mother beside him with her sewing in her lap, and Sissy lay down in her usual spot, on the floor.

The show came on. They watched Jim, Barney, and the rest of the *Mission Impossible* team complete their mission. The final, searing note of the show's theme song ended, and a commercial for Ty-D-Bol came on.

"Daddy," said Sissy. "Tell us about the lynch

mob now."

Ardie sighed. "We don't need to hear that old story again, Sissy. It's time for bed."

"When," asked Ardie's mother, "have you ever been in a hurry to get to bed?"

"I just don't need to hear no stupid ghost stories." Ardie started to rise from her chair.

Her father squinted one eye half-closed and peered at his eldest daughter. "You're not thinkin' you're too old for a ghost story, are you?"

Ardie hesitated. "No." She chose her words carefully. "I'm just tired. I need to get ready for bed."

"You're not scared, are ya?"

"No!"

Sissy said, "Please, Daddy."

"All right." Their father rearranged his seat on the couch, pulling himself more upright and centered. "I'll tell the story, but I'll keep it short, so's Miss Ardie Sue here can get her beauty sleep." He waved his eldest daughter back into her chair.

Everyone's eyes turned to watch the storyteller—even Ardie's.

He took his time before he began, eyelids closed, nodding as if he could hear the words forming in his head. When he spoke, his voice had a low timbre, and the words rolled from his tongue, as if he'd spoken them a thousand times.

"It started so long ago that only the eldest grand-folks remember the days. The last of the generals from both sides of the Civil War were old and dying off, one right after the other. Times were hard, back then. There weren't no money in anybody's pockets. People were stealing bread just to get by—whites and blacks both.

"Folks were poor and gettin' poorer. They were angry at something they couldn't do nothin' about, so they started turning on each other. Back then, it took nothin' more than a bad-cast eye to get a white man angry, and they were runnin' in packs like starvin' wolves. They'd descend on a poor black soul and have him torn to shreds in no time at all."

Sissy bounced a little. "Tell us about the beautiful voodoo priestess."

Her father smiled. "Her name was Bijou, as you well know. She had hair as black as Ardie Sue's and skin colored like hazelnut shells, but her eyes were emeralds that sparkled so bright you could see 'em in the dark. When she spoke, her voice flowed like molasses, with a Lou'siana drawl. She grew up in a family of sharecroppers on a run-down plantation down by Vicksburg, but don't ask me which one. It—and its name—were swallowed up by the waters of the Mississippi, long time ago.

"Now, Bijou had a heart that beat so strong and

clear, it soothed some folks, but got others all riled up. Weren't a soul in the whole county didn't either love or hate that girl. Mostly, it was the white women that hated her, on account o'her beauty. They saw their menfolk looking at her, and it made 'em jealous."

Sissy interjected, "She couldn't help it if she was beautiful."

Her father agreed with a nod, then said, "As you know, the plantation owner had a son named André. Bijou caught André's eye, and he began pursuing her. She pushed him away and avoided him, and when he managed to catch her alone, she gave him whatever excuse she could come up with to keep him from compromisin' her. She knew that even if she went to his bed, he'd never marry her, not with him being white and rich and her being black and a sharecropper. She knew, and she kept away from him for a long time. But the more Bijou rejected André, the more determined he became to have her.

"See, girls, some men, sometimes, want nothing more than to conquer things. It isn't about love. It isn't always even about lust. Sometimes, lots of times, it's about power and controlling and ownership. There's no respect in that, no kindness and, especially, no love, no matter what lies he tells ya to the contrary."

Ardie's father looked pointedly at both girls,

making sure they were listening.

They were.

Sissy said, "So, then André raped her?"

Her father's gaze settled on her, eyelids droop-ing, mouth pulled down, serious. "Who's tellin' this? You? Or me?"

"You are, Daddy."

"That's right." He nodded, slowly, drawing out the pause.

Sissy squirmed.

Finally, he said, "One night, André tricked Bijou into coming to the house. He claimed to be sick and needing Bijou's special healing tea. He was smooth as the snake in the garden, and he had it all planned out. She went to him without suspecting a thing, like a hen wandering into the fox's den. He raped her body, Sissy, yes, but worse, he raped her soul. He took a portion of her sweetness from her that night, and she was never the same. She began to woo voodoo spir-its called the red Loas. She wove her rage into black magic. See, she was a *mambo*, a high priestess.

"She brought a curse down on André, and be-fore long, everyone that lived in the main house had gone crazy. One by one, they killed each other, until they was all dead."

Sissy said, "But not Bijou."

"No. Not Bijou. Not yet. Thing is, when somethin' like that happens, and folks suddenly go crazy and start doing crazy things, people notice, and lots of people noticed what happened to André and his family. They knew somebody was to blame. It didn't take long for them to start pointin' their fingers at Bijou. Even the other sharecroppers were mad at her. By killing the family, she'd shut down the plantation.

"Bijou's mama tried to get her to go away, to move to New Orleans or to St. Louis, but Bijou wouldn't go."

Sissy said, "She'd never been any farther than she could walk from the plantation, not in all her life."

"That's right. She didn't want to leave. It was her home, and so, she stayed."

Sissy pulled her knees to her chest and wrapped her arms around them. "She knew what was comin', right?"

Her father nodded. "Yeah, I reckon she did know what was comin'. But, she also knew there was no way to stop it. See, there was a storm brewin' the likes of which she couldn't control. It had moved in from the Gulf of Mexico and was hitting the Mississippi and Lou'siana coastlines with mean winds and giant waves."

Sissy squeezed her legs tighter. "The hurricane."

"Yes, child. There was one of the worst hurricanes in history coming right up into Mississippi, heading straight for the plantation. Now, the thing about hurricanes and other big storms is that they're more than just storms. The restless dead are attracted to big weather, like hurricanes, and they ride them like the Loas ride the voodoo *mambos*. They're the main reason we take shelter in a storm, 'cause anyone caught out in it, just might...." He paused, then reached over and latched onto Ardie's foot.

Ardie jumped and cried out. So did Sissy. Their mother chuckled, and their father laughed his big, chesty laugh.

"Daddy, don't." Ardie scolded him with a look and pulled her feet up under her.

He gave her arm a teasing shake. "So, Bijou knew this storm was comin', and she knew it would be hungry for souls. When the white men came lookin' for her, she made them chase her out to the riverbank. The wind kicked up, and Bijou reached the end of her breath. She couldn't run anymore."

He leaned forward, resting his elbows on his knees and letting his hands dangle down between. He shook his head slowly from side to side.

"There was six or maybe eight of 'em, eight men coming out of the trees all around Bijou. Bijou's shoes were sinking into the black mud on the riverbank, but she wasn't trying to get away—not anymore. See, Bijou knew that the only way she was going to be free of them was if she let them catch her.

"She let those men come to her. She let them push her down and beat her. With every punch and kick, the storm got bigger. With every angry word, every foul disrespect they threw at her, the hurricane loomed closer. By the time they put the rope around her neck, the rain had started to fall.

"They hanged Bijou, and the wind tossed her body all around at the end of that rope." He flapped his hand in the air to demonstrate. He opened his eyes so wide, the whites nearly glowed in the dim light, and he said, "With her last thoughts, Bijou called on the blackest of all voodoo spirits, Carrefour Ge-Rouge. He came with the hurricane, and he picked up those men on the wind. He tossed them around until they didn't know which way was home. Not a single one of those men was ever seen again, not even their dead bodies."

Ardie's father let a dramatic pause hang in the air. Sissy opened her mouth to interject, but he cut her off with a gesture. "Every now and then...," he said, and Sissy closed her mouth, "people see the ghosts of those men. They're still out there, roaming the riverbanks. Some say they're looking for Bijou, wanting to ask her forgiveness, so they can earn a place in Heaven. Others say they're looking for misbehavin' blacks to punish. Alls I know is, whenever there's a storm, it's best to stay inside. You can hear 'em, in the wind, if you listen real close, calling out to Bijou. You don't want to be out there when they catch up with whoever they're chasin'."

No one spoke for a full thirty seconds. No one moved either, except Ardie's father, who shifted his eyes to look at first one daughter, then the other. They were both listening for the wind.

Their mother broke the silence. "All right, girls. I think it's time to get ready for bed."

Sissy jumped up, put her arms around her father's neck and kissed his cheek. He hugged her to him. "Thanks, Daddy."

"You're welcome, child. No nightmares, now, y'hear me? You're safe inside this house."

"No, no nightmares. Good night." Sissy went to her mother.

Ardie bent to kiss her father. "Good night, Daddy."

He took hold of her forearm and held her there, bent, face to face with him, and he looked into her cinnamon eyes with his own, the color of Mississippi mud, and he said, "Ardie Sue, you're eighteen now. You're practically a woman."

"I know."

"You got to be cautious, girl. There's still plenty out there that you don't understand, and some of those things could hurt you real bad."

"I know. I'm careful. I promise."

"And you watch out for your sister."

"I do." Ardie pulled gently away. She stood upright, then bent to kiss her mother. "Good night."

◆

The next morning, Ardie got up early for church. She helped Sissy put her hair into poodle puffs above each ear. Ardie styled her own after Naomi Sims in a Virginia Slims ad. She picked it out natural in the back and pushed it away from her face with a headband.

Sissy sat on the toilet lid, watching. "You going to meet up with Justin after church?"

Ardie looked at herself in the mirror. "Maybe."

"If you gotta sneak it," Sissy said, repeating one of her mother's sayings, "then it can't come to no good."

Ardie let her have the last word.

The family climbed into the old, Buick Lesabre station wagon, long-since faded from cherry red to rust. Ardie sat in the back seat with Sissy. They looked out their respective windows in silence, all the way to the Baptist church in Greenwood.

Throughout the service, Ardie thought about

Justin. Something in her belly tightened, whenever he crossed her mind. She and Justin had met at a high school football game. The Panthers, Ardie's team, had lost that game. There'd been a fight, and someone had shoved Ardie. Justin had helped her to her feet.

Ardie liked the way Justin looked. He had Italian features, dark hair soft and curly, lightly tanned skin, and eyes that strayed to her body with appreciation.

He said things like, "I can't get you out of my mind, Ardie."

He had offered her a ride home one afternoon, but Ardie had said no. She had known what her father's reaction would be if he had caught her in a white man's truck. The next day, Justin had met her with a plan. "Take the bus, Ardie, but get off at my place. I'll walk you the rest of the way, along the railroad tracks. It's only a couple miles. I'll turn back before we get there, and your papa'll never know. You can just tell him you wanted the walk, which wouldn't be lying."

Ardie had agreed, and it had become a regular thing. Recently, he had asked her to meet him on Sunday afternoon, at two o'clock, at the spot where he usually dropped her off. She had told him she'd be there.

After the service, the congregation took its time

leaving. Everybody needed a conversation with everybody else before they could go home for lunch. The crowd wove in and out of itself, smiles flashing and heads nodding. The ladies clucked and fluttered around, with their big, feathered hats flapping, while the men gathered in stoic groups of two or three, clasping hands and discussing crops and sports.

Ardie's mother joined her family. "Tornados," she said. "In Texas. Worst they ever seen. Lotsa folks missing and dead. Pastor Jones just got a call from his sister, who's a nurse out in Austin. She says the storm hit there this morning, and folks been coming to the hospital all messed up."

"We'll pray for them," Ardie's father said.

"They're saying the storm's coming this way."

"Well, it's got a long way to travel, don't it."

◆

Once lunch was over, Ardie's mother and father got in the Buick and headed off to Aunt Loretta's, making their Sunday rounds. Ardie didn't expect them back for a couple hours. She had already changed from her church clothes into her favorite jeans and blouse. She put on a jacket and headed for the front door.

Sissy caught her in the foyer. "Where you going?"

"Out."

"Mama says we're supposed to stay close to the house."

Ardie zipped her jacket. "I'm not going far. Just for a walk."

"Mama says we're supposed to stick together."

"She did not say that." Ardie gave her sister a disgusted look.

"She said we were supposed to watch out for each other." Sissy's jaw was set and stubborn. "How can I watch out for you, if I don't know where you are?"

"I'm just going out by the railroad tracks. I feel like getting some fresh air." Ardie pushed past.

"Justin gonna be there?"

Ardie hesitated long enough that the answer was obvious.

"He is, ain't he."

"'Ain't' ain't a word." Ardie opened the door and stepped outside. "I'll be back in an hour. Stay outta trouble." She walked up the dirt lane and crossed Money Road. She jumped the ditch and cut through the trees to get to the railroad tracks.

Sumac trees blocked the view from the road on one side, and on the other, fallow fields extended outward for as far as the eye could see. Newly turned rows decorated the dirt expanse. Winter, or its Mississippi changeling, was already gone, and Spring was just around the corner, leaving the state in seasonal limbo.

Ardie measured her steps by the railroad ties, hopping a little to cover the full distance between them. She and Sissy had played on these tracks for as long as she could remember, had found arrow heads and obsidian among the dull, lava rocks. They'd placed pennies on the tracks to be flattened and had contests to see who could walk the rail the farthest without falling off.

Justin hadn't arrived yet.

Ardie paced awhile, then sat on the cold iron rail and picked through the rocks between her feet.

The sky had soured. Clouds sank closer to the earth, bloated with rain. Thunder rolled across the horizon. A single, fat raindrop landed on Ardie's shoulder. She looked up and cursed quietly to herself.

"Ardie!" Justin came trotting through the trees that separated the tracks from the road, pushing his bicycle over the bumpy terrain.

Ardie grinned, wrapped her arms around herself and watched him approach.

"I'm sorry I'm late," he said. "My father was hassling me. He didn't want me to leave the house. We got relatives staying with us, ya know?"

Ardie nodded.

"I snuck out." Justin lay his bike down on its side. "You look pretty today." He tipped his head, and his smile was beguiling.

"Thank you." Ardie followed him to a sheltered spot among the trees. They sat on a lap blanket he had brought with him, rolled and tied to his bike. They sipped from a bottle of grape soda he'd brought.

"I really like you," Justin said. "You like me too?"

Ardie nodded.

He held her hand and told her about his family, about their visitors, his brothers, his job, and, "Can I kiss you?"

Ardie hadn't spoken much, so the sudden question caught her by surprise. While she was trying to think of what to say, he did it. He kissed her.

Ardie didn't pull away. She let him explore her, lick into her mouth and suck on her lips. They kissed for a quarter of an hour. When his hand slid down to her breast, she didn't stop him.

"Am I your boyfriend?" He whispered the question into her ear.

Ardie nodded, woozy and flushed.

He stroked her cheek. "You're my girlfriend," he whispered, then kissed her some more.

When he took her hand and placed it on the

hard lump in his pants, pressing and rubbing himself with her fingers under his, she pulled back.

"It's okay. Don't be afraid. It feels good when you touch me there. I like it. That's what a woman does to a man." He recaptured her mouth. He slid his hand up her thigh and tucked it into the crux between her legs.

Darkening clouds gathered overhead, spectators drawn to the young lovers. They weren't alone.

"What have we here?" asked a man.

Ardie and Justin broke apart.

With her heart in her throat, Ardie looked up to see Mr. Laconi, Justin's father. "Justin, get your ass home. Right now."

"Pop, me and Ardie was just...."

"Now!" The man shouted it and pointed toward the road for emphasis.

Justin leapt to his feet and took off toward his bike.

Ardie scrambled to her feet.

Mr. Laconi grabbed her by the arm. "Not you."

Justin looked over his shoulder, but he didn't stop moving. He stumbled and nearly fell.

"Please, I didn't mean no harm." Ardie could feel the tears burning the backs of her eyes. Her nose tingled with growing upset. "Please." She tried to pull away.

Laconi held on tighter to her arm, bruising her.

"You," he hissed, "will settle down. How do you think your papa would feel if he knew what you been doin'?"

That was the key that freed the tears.

Justin half-ran his bike out to the road. He looked back one more time, face masked with worry. His father pointed again, message clear, and Justin got on his bike and rode toward home.

Laconi watched him go, until he was out of sight, then he lifted Ardie's chin and forced her to look at him. "Now you listen to me, little girl. You make a sound, and I'll tell your papa and your mama that I found you out here with Justin. You be quiet, and be a good girl, and it'll be our little secret, okay?"

Ardie nodded. For a split second, she had the thought that everything would be okay.

But then, he said, "Sit down." He followed her down to the blanket. "You smell good. I can see why Justin was so turned on by you. You're a fine mouthful." He slid his hand down the front of her body, over a breast then down her belly. It came to rest at the juncture of her legs. "This what you like?"

Ardie pushed his hand away.

"No, no," he crooned, dipping his face into the curve of her neck. "That's not how this is gonna work." He tucked his hand up inside her shirt instead, to her breast, working up under her bra. "Don't worry. I'm not gonna hurt ya. You and me are gonna be good friends."

Ardie squirmed. "I need to get home." She didn't like the way he smelled—of tooth decay and cow dung.

Laconi looked her in the eyes. "Not yet. Just a little bit longer, okay? Please? I'm gonna show you what it's like to be with a real man." He rolled her nipple. "You're gonna like it."

"Please," Ardie whimpered. Her tears flowed more profusely.

"That's a good girl." Laconi reached down and undid the button on her jeans.

Ardie didn't know what to do.

He pushed his hand into her pants, fingers sliding across her pubic mound.

"Stop it!" Ardie grabbed his wrist. She squeezed her thighs together and squirmed, trying to get away from him.

He forced his hand deeper. "Shh," he said, but he lost all pretense of tenderness. He grabbed her by the neck with his other hand, thumb pressed painfully across her Adam's apple.

Ardie let out a strangled cry.

"It's okay," Laconi said. Then, he focused all his attention on his fingertips and delved deeper into her pants. "Stop fighting me, girl. It's okay. I'm not gonna hurt ya." He was big and strong, a farmer who had spent his life hefting hundred-pound bags of seed.

Ardie was no match for him. Her sobs became her only means of protest.

"That's right," Laconi said.

Ardie felt him touch her where no man had ever done before. At the same time, her hand closed on a large rock, and before the thought had even entered her conscious mind, she was swinging it.

The wind kicked up.

Ardie hit Laconi in the head.

He fell back, hand still stuck in her jeans, pulling Ardie over onto him. She tugged his arm free and crawled backwards away from him. She brandished the rock out in front of her, ready to hit him again if necessary.

He looked stunned, half-lying, half-sitting. He was breathing through his open mouth, brow furrowed, eyes closed, and holding his head.

A different voice, one sweet to Ardie's ears, called, "Ardie Sue!" Sissy was walking down the tracks toward them. The wind buffeted her and whipped her coat around her legs.

Ardie welcomed the sight with such relief that she nearly collapsed. She let her hand and the rock in it fall to the ground. Simultaneously, the clouds let loose, and rain came down in fat, wet splashes.

"You bitch," said Laconi. He had a slim line of

blood running from his hairline down his cheek.

Ardie heard the intention in his voice, saw the anger and the violence in his eyes. Before she could react, however, he rolled over and grabbed her arm.

Laconi's hand closed on the same, bruised spot where he'd held her before.

Ardie cried out in pain.

"Ardie Sue!" Sissy was running toward them now.

Laconi looked up and saw Sissy. He watched the approaching girl. "That your sister?" He didn't wait for an answer. He got to his feet and dragged Ardie up with him. He walked her to the tracks and stood there, waiting, holding Ardie by the arm.

Sissy stopped several feet away. She was panting and wild-eyed.

"C'mere, girl," said Laconi. "Your sister's hurt. She fell down on the rocks. I was trying to help her, but now you're here."

At that moment, Ardie understood just how serious the situation had become. The pain in her arm and throat were nothing compared to the pain in her heart at the thought of what Laconi might do to Sissy.

In a split second, Ardie made a decision. She yelled, "Run, Sissy!" and kicked Laconi as hard as she could. She bent and bit into his hand.

Laconi let out a yowl. He jerked Ardie hard, almost knocking her off her feet.

"Run, Sissy! Get Daddy!"

But Sissy didn't run away. She ran at Laconi. She extended her arms and plowed into him, shoving him back a step or two.

Laconi would have recovered quickly from the small girl's attack, but for the lava rocks on the tracks. He lost his footing and started to fall backwards. He took Ardie with him, and the two of them tumbled down the short incline. In the tangle, Laconi released Ardie's arm.

As soon as she could, Ardie got to her feet. Her only thought was escape. She stumbled back toward Sissy.

"Run!" Ardie grabbed her sister by the hand and took off down the tracks.

Sissy ran with her. "What's going on?"

"Nothing."

"Why'd you hit him?"

"Just run, Sissy!"

The rain came down harder. It held nothing back. It was a vengeful rain.

Ardie looked back over her shoulder in time to see Laconi take off toward the road.

"We gotta get across the road," Ardie cried. "Now!" She headed into the trees by the road. She knew Laconi would be able to cut them off, if he got to his truck.

As soon as their feet hit the blacktop, Ardie saw Laconi coming up the road in his black, Ford pick-up, engine roaring. His face, behind the windshield wipers, was furious.

Sissy screamed, and they ran across the road.

Laconi swerved toward them.

They leapt across the ditch and entered the field on the other side.

Laconi skidded to a stop behind them.

Ardie noticed how dark it had gotten. Clouds formed a shroud overhead, effectively cutting them off from the security of sunlight. They had to run into the wind and driving rain. The storm was coming from the northwest, the direction of home.

A dead branch broke free from a tree and flew across the field in front of them. As they passed the abandoned Macon house, shingles flew off its roof and careened through the air like magic carpets that had lost their drivers.

"C'mon," shouted Ardie, shielding her eyes with her arm. She headed for the riverbank.

"Where you going?" Sissy jerked her sister's hand.

"Down by the river. The trees'll shelter us. We can... cut up toward the house... the back way."

Sissy grabbed Ardie's arm and halted her. "No,

Ardie!"

Ardie immediately looked back to see where Laconi was. He was maneuvering his truck into the field, bumping down into the ditch.

Sissy cried, "We can't go down by the river. That's where the lynch mob is."

"Don't be stupid! He's coming after us, and he'll kill us if he catches us." Ardie pulled her sister onward. She ran as fast as she could make Sissy go. They crossed the open field toward the band of trees that lined the Tallahatchie River.

Lightning lit the sky, and thunder came right on its heels, sharply assaulting their eyes and ears.

Ardie knew Sissy was terrified of storms. "Just look at the ground. Keep your eyes on the ground ahead of you, and don't stop until we get home."

Three-quarters of the way across the field, Sissy had lost her breath, and the weight of the rain and wind was taking its toll.

Ardie slowed and put her arm around Sissy's waist. "C'mon! We can make it. I know we can."

Sissy gasped for air.

The sound of a revving engine came from behind them. Ardie looked back to see Laconi's truck bouncing and jumping across the field. It could only go so fast, but it was gaining on them.

"C'mon!" Ardie half-carried her sister the rest

of the way, and at last, they reached the trees. As Ardie had predicted, the copse provided shelter from the wind, but it held other hazards. They had to slow down even more.

The sisters followed the riverbank. The water of the Tallahatchie was distressed.

Ardie knew that if Laconi wanted to follow them there, he'd have to do so on foot.

Then, she heard them—men's voices, echoing. They sounded far away, coming from a direction that wasn't part of Ardie's world. She couldn't make out the words, but they sounded like the baying of dogs on the hunt, hungry and eager.

"Y'hear that?" Ardie's breath burned her throat.

Sissy didn't reply. She had her hands over her ears and her chin to her chest.

Ardie began to see shadows and movement out of the corners of her eyes. She had a stitch in her side, but she kept going, pushing aside branches with one arm and supporting Sissy with the other.

She became aware of a roar. She was sure it was Laconi in his black truck. She cast a glance over her shoulder and saw she was wrong. It was a twister, on the other side of the river, less than a mile away. It was dropping down out of the clouds like a devil's tongue, lashing around, tasting the air. It kicked up a swirling dust cloud in which larger things spun and toppled. Ardie had never seen one so big. She stopped in her tracks and watched it, mesmerized.

Sissy stuck herself up against Ardie, trembling fiercely, body racked with ragged breath. "I hear 'em, Ardie! I hear... the lynch mob! They're in the storm!"

Ardie heard them too, and still, she said, "There's no such thing as ghosts."

Men's angry voices cut through the gale. "You can't run fast enough!" And, "We'll teach you 'bout respect!" And, "You done forgot yer place, little girl!"

Ardie pushed her sister ahead of her. "Go on, Sissy! Go!"

The rain beat against them, flying nearly horizontal along with a mix of dirt and rocks and twigs that cut their exposed skin. The twister raged toward them, getting louder and louder in each passing moment.

Sissy turned and ran, arms in front of her face, head down. "They're comin'!"

Ardie barely heard her sister over the voices bellowing in her head. They were all around her now, all around, all hateful. Every rock that bruised her body, every stick that cut into her flesh, was a blow from them. They knew her name, and they called it as they closed in. They wanted her. They hungered for her, for Ardenia Sue Johnson.

Ardie remembered what her daddy had said

about Bijou. He'd said she had lost a piece of her
sweetness that day, the day André had raped her.
He'd said she had called on Carrefour Ge-Rouge, the
blackest of the voodoo spirits, to make the men pay.

Ardie dared a look over her shoulder.

Laconi came crashing through the trees with a
rope in his hand. His eyes glowed with the fever of
hate. He paid no attention to the cuts on his face. The
lynch mob rode him like the loas ride mambos, like
they ride storms. He had become their storm.

Ardie knew he wouldn't give up, couldn't give
up. She also knew he couldn't hurt them both at the
same time.

"Run, Sissy! Run home!"

Ardie watched Sissy charge on ahead, but she
didn't follow. She let him come, let them come.

Sissy disappeared into the trees.

"Run, Sissy! There's no such thing as...."

The wind swallowed the rest of her words and
every other sound but its own roar.

Ardie turned and faced Mr. Laconi.

His face was split in a cruel grin, and when he
saw that she wasn't running, he slowed down too.
He was limping. When he got close enough, he said,
"Your sister can't save you. Your daddy can't save you.
I'm gonna make sure you never speak another word."

He made a grab for her, but Ardie instinctually

took a step back.

"C'mere!" he shouted. He lurched forward, and this time, he managed to latch onto a handful of Ardie's hair. He drew her in tight against his body. "Good girl." He started shaking out the rope.

Ardie felt blows all over her body. Something hit her hard in the arm. Something else slammed into her leg and nearly knocked her off her feet. The wind crashed around them, tearing apart trees. A fat branch flew by, as if it were a twig. Ardie squinted against the sharp rain.

Laconi wrapped the rope around Ardie's neck.

Desperate, Ardie cried, "Bijou!" She shouted it at the top of her lungs. "Bijou!" She got out only two before Laconi started to squeeze the rope tight. Ardie began to choke. She felt her head swelling. Her lungs ached. Her throat was being crushed. Dizziness came, then a blackness that seeped in at the edge of her vision.

She felt a sudden jerk on the rope that pulled her off her feet. It tugged her up, then let her fall. She came down on her side in the mud. As darkness closed in, she saw Laconi flying backwards, into the air, up and way into a swirling mass of debris. He was screaming, though Ardie only knew that because of how his face contorted.

Ardie closed her eyes. The darkness had become

complete.

A gentle voice spoke in Ardie's ear. "Ardenia Sue." The woman drew out her vowels. It felt like a dream. "Ardenia Sue, go home."

Ardie gradually became aware of her surroundings. She was alone, lying on the ground with a rope around her neck. The wind still howled, but in the distance. The storm had moved on.

◆

*Years later, on a stormy night, Ardenia Sue gathers her children around herself. She tells them a story about two young girls. She tells them about the evil man that chased them. She tells them how the oldest girl saved her sister's life and how an emerald-eyed ghost made everything all right. Never once does she mention skin color, because it doesn't make the story any scarier, and when she pauses, lost in memory, the children listen for the wind.*

————◆◆————

# The Daughter

## 1

Death did not leave alone. The daughter was standing at the hearth, slicing roots into the stew, contemplating the fact that the harvest had lasted, and she acknowledged her own gratitude thereof.

The crude carving the father had made of the harvest woman stood upon the mantle. Many years prior, the father had placed it there and, throughout the dark seasons, he had made offerings of wheat and meat to it.

The blood stew—a mixture of mutton, carrots, beets, potatoes, and onions—looked almost black as it began to boil. Its earthy aroma blossomed, and sheep fat rose to the surface, swirling in patterns. Its twining lured the daughter into a trance. Oily spirals flowed in and out of one another with no beginning and no end. In the patterns, the daughter saw meaning, and dread birthed in her belly. Something terrible was about to happen.

The daughter leaned close and focused on interpreting the omens. Among them, she saw a rambling landscape from a crow's eye view. Then, the signs shifted and curled into the face of a crone, then they changed again.

Deaf, the daughter did not hear him approach.

A hand wrapped around her upper arm and jerked her around.

Disoriented and disturbed by her visions, the daughter raised her arms to protect herself. The blade in her hand, forgotten, cut upward.

It seemed, at first, as if there were no harm done. It was only the father, irritated at having to cross the room to get the daughter's attention. Because she'd been standing on the hearth, she hadn't felt the vibrations when he'd banged his staff against the floor.

But then, the father faltered. He had his hand to his neck. His mouth moved, forming shapes, now tight, now wide. Blood leaked through the father's fingers, and his eyes held fear. He clutched at the daughter.

She helped him to his fur-covered bed, where he lay gasping like a fish pulled from the stream. The father's blood flowed from the wound without cease. It soaked into his bed furs and straw. It filled the small hut with its groundwater aroma. He grew pale and still, but he didn't take his eyes off the daughter.

Choked by fear, the daughter remembered the

old sow, slaughtered at first snow. It had given her that same, wild-eyed look.

The daughter dropped to her knees beside the father. She looked him in the eyes, shook her head tightly, and wished she could make him understand that she hadn't done it on purpose; he had startled her.

As his life drained away, tears ran down her cheeks. She remained vigilant for the moment when Death would turn away and let him live, because she loved him and because the break in his skin had been her fault.

## 2

Far away, Bródir stood naked at the entrance to his hut, looking out across the cold, stony landscape of Ellan Vannin and the sea beyond. Dawn's burgeoning light cast gray into the night sky. Bródir shivered. His woman slept still, but Bródir had been awakened by his own sense of anticipation. His fate loomed, prickly, at the back of his head. He considered the importance of the moment and went over all the details in his mind, the condition of his armor and weapons, and the state of his men. His ships waited in the harbor to take them all off to war.

## 3

The daughter buried the father in a spot where the morning sun would warm his bones. It was a shallow grave, on which she arranged a layer of rocks stolen from the pasture wall. For seven days, from dawn to dusk, she stayed beside him, crying within her silence. She arranged and re-arranged the stones. She lay on the unforgiving earth beside him and waited for someone to come for her or for an omen to tell her what to do.

Eventually, she returned to her routine and found solace in its familiarity. It wasn't much, but it was something. She added the father's chores to her own. She carried water and cared for the animals. At first, she wasted more food than she ate by making enough for two, out of habit. She needed no voice to pray for deliverance from her loneliness.

Planting season was upon the land, but she hadn't the strength required for turning the soil. With each passing day, her stores of roots and herbs grew leaner. She ate less and feared more. She told herself that the harvest woman had abandoned her because she'd been unable to read the omens in the stew, and so she watched for more signs, determined not to miss them again.

A cat came and lived with her for a while. She

shared her food with it and consoled her soul with the animal's companionship. It slept beside her, its warm body thrumming as she petted it for hours.

Then, one evening, the cat didn't return.

The daughter stood at the threshold throughout the night, willing it home.

She found its half-eaten remains at morning light, its entrails dragged from it.

A smaller hump of dirt and rocks joined the other. The daughter cried no less for the cat than she had for the father. Alone again, she kept a vigil by the graves and prayed in the only way she knew how.

That first night, she fell asleep with her arm draped over the cat's stones and awoke from a nightmare. A mist was falling, covering her and the graves with a clinging blanket of cold. She rose and went inside. The nightmare followed her there because she didn't even try to reject it.

In it, she was standing in a field of graves. For as far as her eye could see, the ground was rumpled with piles of stones and earth. Large and small, they surrounded her on all sides. She stood alone at the center, and an upswell of emotion like none she'd ever known overcame her. It clenched her throat and cut off her air. It filled her eyes with brine, blurring her vision. Her head ached, and her face tensed to bursting.

The daughter took the nightmare to bed with her, holding it close beneath the furs. She couldn't stop thinking about the moment in the dream when she'd opened her mouth and released her anxiety, fear, and sorrow. Her anguish had swarmed from her like bees from a hive—the unabashed squall of the child she had once been.

## 4

Bródir and his brother Óspak stood shoulder to shoulder at the prow of the drekkar. The Viking dragon ship cut cleanly through the water, followed by an army of longships. They passed morning-side of the island Yn Cholloo, heading southward along the Irish coast. They traveled to join the King of Leinster in a massive battle against Brian Bóraimhe, the Emperor of Ireland.

Óspak gazed out at the cold sea. "The wind blows foul. The old ways are dying, and the Christians have arrived with force. It's a time of change. We must embrace it or die along with the old gods."

"No, brother. The wind blows fair." Bródir captured his long black hair at the nape of his neck and braided it. "I'll have my fate from this battle. Brian will fall, and I will rise in his place."

"You?" Óspak cast him a sidelong look.

"You doubt me?"

"You have others besides Brian to stand in your way." Óspak tucked his thumbs into the arm-holes of his chainmail shirt and lifted the heavy armor an inch off his vast shoulders. He held it there and flexed his neck from side to side.

Bródir watched Óspak with half-lidded, steely eyes. "Oh?"

"Sigurd the Stout may have something to say about it."

"Well, he won't get my ear until we're both in the Halls of Valhöl." Bródir pulled the long braid through his waist-belt, to anchor it against the tugging wind.

"That may be true, brother." The chainmail shirt dropped back into place with a rolling whisper of metal on metal. "But, if I were you...," Óspak turned to walk away, "...I wouldn't count on his being the first to arrive." As he passed, he slipped two fingers under his brother's braid and lifted it free of the belt. The wind took it and unraveled it.

## 5

One morning, the daughter packed a bundle, tidied the hut, cried one last time with the father, and—following the omens—she walked off into the countryside. The food had run out. The chickens and yearling pigs had all been slaughtered. The root cellar was empty.

The daughter's every step landed only by virtue of her determination. For three nights, she slept under the open sky, and for three days, she walked. Spring had come to the island and, with it, more rain. The world had gone colorless. The sky bowed under its own weight, heavy and bloated.

Her wool dress hung damp against her, smelling of wet sheep—a not-entirely unpleasant aroma. Her toes, cold and wrinkling in the father's leather boots, chafed and soured. She sought protection inside the deep hood of her cape, but the wind threw rain at her in gusts, and so her cheeks and eyelashes took on droplets that mingled and ran down her face. The daughter kept walking.

A stream ran along a gully. It wasn't deep, and it wasn't fast. It consumed the raindrops into it matter-of-factly, with neither eagerness nor complaint. The daughter followed it for some distance, skirting around boggy flats and stands of cattails.

When she first saw the woman, she thought she was looking at a cinnabar blanket that had caught upon a bramble. But then, the cloth moved, and it was a woman crouching at the edge of the stream, covered from head to toe in the color of dried blood. The woman held a lichen-purple gown and was pushing it down into the water, drowning it there, then letting the slow current lift and spread the fabric upon its surface.

The woman turned at the sound of approaching footsteps, and it was a crone, old and bent.

Their gazes met, and a band closed around the daughter's heart, making the organ work hard to keep beating. She felt her pulse, like a throb, in the middle of her forehead.

The crone's eyes were as black as a crow's and unblinking. She lifted her chin and stared out across the rolling landscape.

In the distance, two hillocks—little more than mounds—stood side-by-side. The rain made their outlines shimmer and shift. One had a copse of trees upon it. The other was capped with a graveyard or a ruined house.

The daughter brought her attention back to the riverbank, and the crone was gone.

Approaching the place where the crone had been, the daughter saw footprints in the mud. She gathered wildflowers and placed them there in gratitude for the omen, for the daughter was convinced that an omen it had been.

She crossed the stream at a broad and rocky expanse, ignoring the flashes of fish and placing each footfall carefully upon solid rock. When she reached the far side, she turned her steps toward the pair of mounds that the crone had revealed to her.

## 6

Two, long days—spent on the drekkar, rowing from sunrise to sundown and sleeping on wooden benches throughout the night—blended into a night of encampment in a meadow, near the shoreline, north of Cluain Tarbh. Bródir kept his men to one side, and Óspak kept his to the other. The two army leaders met with Máel Mórda mac Murchada, the King of Leinster, one of several Irish kings who opposed Brian's plan to unite Ireland with Brian himself as emperor.

"Brian marches on us," said Máel Morda. Sprawled across a pile of furs and sheepskins, he sucked at his teeth and then took a long draught of mead.

Bródir was carving a toothpick from a twig. "He believes we'll drop our tails and run from him, if he growls at us."

"He believes," corrected Óspak, "that he cannot lose. Tomorrow is Holy Friday, when Brian and his Christians mark the martyring of their god. It will fill them with blood-lust."

"Good," snapped Bródir. "Then, they'll run

at our blades with enthusiasm." He looked to Máel Morda. "How many follow his banner?"

"Fewer than do mine. Fewer by more than a thousand men."

"Then," said Bródir, "we'll be victorious."

Máel Morda grinned. "Aye."

Óspak said nothing more.

Before the sun had risen above the horizon, the sounds of shouts and clanking armor cut through the morning drizzle. The men and allies of Leinster prepared for battle. The plan was set, and word had spread that they would soon engage the army of the Emperor of Ireland.

In the chaos of getting seven thousand armored men into position, Óspak stole away with a thousand of them. He and the Manx warriors that had come with him returned to their ships and continued onward, to Dublin, where they swore fealty to Brian, and where Óspak was baptized into the Christian faith.

Bródir didn't realize his brother's treachery until later that day, when he stepped among the bodies of Óspak's men wearing Brian's mark.

It was at that point that Bródir himself put on Brian's mark and fled south toward Dublin.

# 7

At the edge of the first mound, the daughter came across a cow. It was an uneven mix of black and white. It had angular hips and a wide snout. Its tail hung limp and tired. Its ears flicked with each raindrop that fell upon them. Head low, the cow took several bites of grass. Then, it lifted its head. It stared at the daughter from under thick eyelashes, with its unblinking, black, cow eyes; and it chewed its cud.

The daughter paid it ample attention, letting her gaze drift over the patterns made by white and black on its body. The swirls in the cow's hair held mysteries she sought to understand.

The cow let out a long, mournful bawl that the daughter could only see, not hear, then it looked up the hillock.

It wasn't much, but it was something. The daughter looked too. A stand of trees capped the mound like a crown. Rowan trees, their budding branches slim and fanned out, stood rooted in the hillside just beyond explosions of broom and gorse.

The daughter gathered bundles of sweet clover from the rocks and offered them to the cow.

She climbed the hill. She had lost weight and strength. Her legs ached, and her stomach cramped with hunger, but she pushed onward until she arrived at the rowan trees. The rise grew steeper, and the daughter used the trees to pull herself upward.

She caught movement out of the corner of her eye.

A wolf stood there, watching her, drool running from its bared gums.

The daughter bent and picked up a stick. She menaced the beast with it, then turned and ran up the hill, clutching at tree after tree. Her breath burned in her chest, and it felt as if a knife had been buried in her ribs. She didn't stop until she had reached the clearing at the hill's apex. Gasping, she leaned against a rowan. She could run no farther; she didn't have the strength. She looked this way, that way, and behind. She glanced all around, searching for the wolf, but it was nowhere to be seen.

She stumbled into the clearing and saw that an ancient menhir had been placed there, its face pock-marked and moss-stained. She sat with her back to the stone and rested her head against its cool surface. The vibrations of generations came through the stone where her skull connected with it. She lifted her eyes to the edge of the trees and there she saw the wolf.

Half-cast in shadows, it had all the qualities of a nightmare, its fur sleek and the color of a midnight sky. It was huge and hardy.

The wolf stared at the daughter with its black,

black eyes, and then it was gliding toward her on silent paws, through the stillness of the daughter's world.

The daughter hadn't the strength of body or will. She watched it come, her eyes locked with its, her heart beating big enough to make her whole being throb. She felt the swell inside her. The bees wanted out, but they would not find release. Not then. Not there.

At the last moment, the daughter lifted her hands to shield herself, but it was no use.

The wolf leapt the last four feet, eager to taste the daughter's flesh.

## 8

Bródir crouched down behind a hazel bush.

The battle had raged for a full day in the forest at Cluain Tarbh. Blood stained the trunks of every tree. The stench had thickened throughout the course of the day, as the dying bled into the earth, the dead evacuated bowels and bladders one last time, and the living overturned their stomachs upon the mutilated bodies of their brothers.

Only a handful of Bródir's men remained alive, though the battle raged on. Máel Morda's warriors continued to fight like madmen, as if they'd lost all reason and awareness of loss. Bródir, on the other hand, understood where to find the path of sanity, or so he thought. It led away from this war. Fleeing turned out to be both easier and harder than Bródir expected.

# 9

The daughter stood over herself, no longer cold, sore, hungry, or frightened, but still deaf, still trapped in the world with which she was most familiar. She was unaware that she was missing anything at all.

She watched the wolf gorge itself on her organs, and she waited for someone to come for her or for an omen to tell her where to go.

The wolf sat back and cleaned itself. Its rhythmic licking lulled the daughter into a thoughtless, timeless emptiness. When eventually, the wolf walked into the forest, shadows engulfed it.

The daughter stood in one place. She had no urge to sit, no tiredness in her legs, and no restlessness to make her fidget. The world had become a place of waiting as well as a place of silence, and so, she waited.

## 10

The portents of the day called for the death of a king, but Bródir never would have guessed that he'd be the one to draw the blade across Emperor Brian Bóraimhe's neck.

Fate had drawn him there, Bródir told himself. He had not set out to find the emperor's tent. He'd been fleeing, abandoning his men and allies. But find it he did, and given the opportunity, he seized it.

Brian was kneeling in a tent, in prayer. Before he could finish his Holy Friday ritual, Bródir had slit his throat.

## 11

The crow landed on the ancient stone in the center of the clearing.

The daughter turned her head to see it more clearly. It was her first movement in hours.

With a dancing sway, the bird dug its beak into the moss on the stone, then lifted its head and looked intently at the daughter. Its eyes were the blackest of black.

In those eyes, the daughter saw it. She saw, and she knew intuitively that the crow was the wolf, was the cow, and was the crone. The knowledge did not startle her.

When the crow flew from the stone to her shoulder, the daughter barely moved. She wasn't afraid, and it felt pleasant having the bird perched on her.

Shifting from one taloned foot to the other, the crow kneaded the ethereal matter of her being.

The daughter liked that too. It didn't tickle, but it didn't hurt either. It wasn't much, but it was something.

Then, the crow flew away.

Before the daughter could resist or even question it, she found herself flying through the air as naturally as if she had always known how to do it. Her first inclination was to look down, and she saw the hills, the farms, and the rivers. Her second inclination was to look up, and that, she found, pleased her more. The clouds looked different from there, bigger and more sculpted, and the rain that splashed her face didn't feel nearly as heavy as it had on the ground.

She flew in the crow's wake, and the landscape scrolled by far below.

Gradually, the smell of slaughter reached her. The daughter had no experience with war. At first, she knew only confusion when she saw the bodies scattered below. In the distance, fires burned, binding earth to sky with thick bands of smoke.

The crow veered downward and perched on a

branch near a noble tent. The daughter followed. She landed on the ground with grace.

A man, dressed in armor and covered with the bloodstains of battle, stood looking into the tent, strangely immobile. People ran all around, urgent and tragic.

The daughter felt drawn to the man, as if her fate were woven with his.

The man had a long, black braid that he tucked into his waist-belt at the back. It had become ragged during his battles. Carefully and slowly, he withdrew a large dagger from its sheath.

He glanced over his shoulder, and the daughter got a look at his filthy, handsome face. She saw steely eyes and the triumph in them.

Then, the warrior slipped into the tent.

The throbbing started. It shook the daughter's entire body. She felt as if she would burst with grief, a torment far worse than any she had felt at the loss of the father. It churned her guts and roiled in her chest. The pressure continued to build. It straightened her spine and pushed up her chin. It forced her mouth open, and she keened.

Every sorrow poured out of her, until she felt her eyes would burn from their sockets with the intensity of it. She wailed and wallowed in death—her father's, her own, the warriors', and the Emperor's.

The bees poured from her. She drained herself without ever hearing her own cries.

A woman crashed out of the tent, face exploding with terror. Before she could release the tent flap, however, a strong hand grabbed her by the hair and wrenched her back. A blade slid across her throat. It released a scarlet flow of blood that ran down her chest and stained her lichen-purple gown. She fell onto her back, and the man in the tent dragged her inside.

## 12

Bródir put as much distance as he could between himself and the dead emperor's tent. He ran for a long time, until his legs wobbled and his lungs burned. He heard the first calls near dawn. They had surrounded him. He watched as they came through the trees. Brian Bóraimhe's brother was in the lead, and he had murder in his eyes.

## 13

The daughter awoke upon the ancient stone in the hilltop clearing. She felt the itchy crawl along her spine and the welling of sorrow that had awakened her. She had to go to him, just as she had had to follow the omens. Her destiny had brought her to it. Her life had prepared her for it.

The crow sat nearby, preening its feathers. It watched and waited.

This time, the daughter didn't need the crow to lead her. With her eyes lifted to the sky, she flew up and turned instinctually toward the one whose fate was summoning her. She knew where to go without knowing.

The crow followed her.

Far below, in the forest north of Dublin, the daughter saw a handful of warriors surrounding a poor soul who had come to the end of his days. She dove slowly toward him, watching from above as they made him walk around and around a tree.

The man who needed her—the warrior from the tent—lifted his face and bit at the sky.

A large soldier hit the man. Others threw rocks and made him keep circling.

A bloody cord connected him to the tree, a thick rope of intestine. His captors had opened the man's gut. Forced to walk, he gradually wound his own entrails around the trunk, pulling them from his body one bloody step at a time. But still, he snapped and growled like a cornered wolf.

The daughter put foot to earth nearby, within sight of the tortured man. Her discomfort grew. His death approached, and when she could hold it back no longer, she opened her mouth and released her bees.

The man's chin came up as if someone had grasped his long, black braid and jerked his head back. His mouth opened, and he joined the daughter with his own outpouring of pain and fury. When he'd expended the last of his breath, his body gave out, and nothing the other men said or did would get him back on his feet. He was dead.

## 14

The daughter lost consciousness in the midst of the wailings and awoke back at the stone. She remained there until the itch called her out to attend another death. The harvest woman visited the daughter, sometimes as the crow, sometimes as the crone, wolf, or cow, though she came less often as time progressed. The daughter needed her less.

In time, the daughter forgot the father and the farm. She came to crave the wailing for its release and its purpose. She liked having a purpose. It wasn't much, but it was something.

——◆◆◆——

# The Haunting of Mrs. Poole

The Charred Lady first appeared to me on July 2, 1872. My wedding gown haunted me that night, hanging from a nail on the wall. It glowed in the lamplight and hovered in the periphery of my vision, a ghost reminding me my life was about to change. I was to be married on the morrow, to become Mrs. Orton Poole.

It had been an exhausting day of forced smiles, handshakes, and toasts. Having been raised in an orphanage in Richmond, Virginia, I was not accustomed to boisterous celebrations with the well-to-do. I had tumbled through conversation as a sea urchin tumbles in a surging tide pool.

Finally, I found sanctuary in my room, rereading portions of *Critique of Pure Reason* by the German philosopher Immanuel Kant. My beloved tutor, Mr. Smith, had uncovered my talents for Mathematics, Philosophy, and Metaphysics, a combination that had led him to introduce me to Herr Kant's bold thoughts. I have since read everything the philosopher ever wrote. If the man hadn't died before my birth, he'd have found himself burdened, I fear, with an admirer. Thus, I was grateful for the time alone with my thoughts and his.

The day had sweltered, and the oncoming night promised equal discomfort. I opened the window to let in whatever dogged breeze could find its way to me. Poole Manor, my future home, wasn't the most hospitable of buildings, and the narrow window granted me only a sliced view of the grounds. The scent of sweet magnolia rose from the lawn below, and from my vantage on the second floor, I saw fireflies twinkling on the bank of the James River, against a backdrop of black water.

That's when I saw her, standing on the lawn, cast in shadows. At first I thought it must be one of Orton's servants, but no, not in such an elegant hooded cloak. A wedding guest, perhaps?

She stepped into the moonlight.

She was deformed. Her features tipped askew as if mottled by so many scars they no longer sat right upon her cheekbones. This became more apparent as she lifted her chin to look at me. Our gazes locked, and I gasped in horror to see she had only one eye, the other's removal having left an empty socket. She made no attempt to cover her hideousness but faced me as if daring me to see her.

I stumbled back from the window, eager to be

free of her scrutiny, and as I watched, the glass on the open window frosted from the bottom upward, crystalline and white, spreading like blanched roots up the pane. The room grew cold.

I wrapped my arms around myself, wanting to scream...but incapable in the moment.

Written by a ghostly finger, letters appeared in the frost. It started with a cursive T, and my mind followed each developing curve. It spelled, "Too many mouths."

I did scream then, and fainted, or near to it. By the time I came back to myself, my sister was bending over me, and the frost had gone, taking its strange message with it.

"You poor darlin'," said Anna. She was seventeen, two years younger than I. Anyone of sound sight and mind could have guessed we were sisters. We both had the same ginger hair, hazel eyes, and heart-shaped, freckled face.

She was practical, whereas I had the soul of a philosopher and mathematician. It was always she who reminded me mealtime had arrived or that I was due in the chapel for prayers. I would have starved of body and soul, lost in my books and calculations, if it hadn't been for her.

Anna helped me off the floor. "Have your nerves become unbearable?"

I laughed with her and decided not to mention the woman or the frost. Kant's words echoed across my mind: *I had therefore to remove knowledge, in order to make room for belief.* I was not ready to believe in apparitions.

"Don't you worry about anything, dearest Amelia," my sister said. "All you need is a good night's rest. Tomorrow's a big day." She assisted me with my dressing gown and tucked me into bed.

I watched her turn down the lamp and move toward the door.

"Anna," I called at the last minute, giving in to my weakness. "Stay here with me tonight. Will you, please? Like when we were little? After tomorrow—"

"Of course," she said, changing direction and returning to the bed. She lay her robe on a chair, then crawled in with me.

"After tomorrow," she whispered, "you won't want to sleep with your sister; you'll have a man to give you babies."

We giggled together for a while, talked about how we wished our parents had survived to see the day, and eventually fell asleep.

By the time I awoke, Anna had returned to her own room. I rolled to look at the indent her body had left in the linens, already mourning a childhood in which she had been my one true light. She could have

stayed at the orphanage where we'd spent the previ-
ous decade, but I'd insisted Orton allow her to live
with us. With his contacts and wealth, we could bring
her out into Richmond society and find her a good
husband.

As I lay there, I noticed a bit of black sticking
out from under her pillow, the end of a velvet ribbon.
I pushed up on one elbow and pulled it out. Anna had
forgotten her cameo choker. It had been our mother's.

I was shocked by its state. It was battered,
stained with a dark substance that had seeped into
cracks I'd never noticed before. The cameo itself was
the profile of a woman, but her nose had broken off,
and it struck me that her eye was just a carved hole.

Remembering the Charred Lady, I shivered,
and it was enough to push me out of bed. I replaced
the memory with activity. It was, after all, my wedding day, and I had many preparations to make.

When Anna came to help me dress and arrange
my hair, I asked her as gently as I could about the
choker. "How did it get so damaged?"

Anna stared at it in horror, took it in her own
two hands and turned it over. She trembled, on the
verge of tears. "I don't know," she said. "Where did
you find it?"

"It was here, under the pillow, this morning."

Shaking her head, she turned toward the door.

"This can't be mine. Who would do this?" She hurried from the room with me on her heels.

She went straight to her jewelry box, and I saw over her shoulder that her own cameo was there, the perfect twin of the ruined one. It wasn't cracked, and its black velvet ribbon was pristine. She turned a grin on me. "There? You see? You scared me for nothing. This isn't mine."

She handed the stained and dirtied one back to me. I stared down at it wondering how there could be two of them, so alike, and yet with such different stories.

Upon returning to my room, I tucked the mysterious choker in a trinket box and put it out of my mind in favor of bridal bliss.

◆

"Are you crying?" There was no tenderness in the question.

I couldn't answer either.

"Stop it. This is what you were created for. God put Woman on this Earth so Man could make babies in her. You are my wife now. This is your duty."

I nodded, but the tears continued to flow as Orton, my husband, positioned himself between my legs. I had the urge to shove him away, to hit him in the face, and to flee, but I did not. I had made my bargain. I was his wife. The finality of it hit me.

"Stop crying, I say. Obey me. Or cover your head. I don't care to see it. It's weakening my resolve."

He pulled the sheet over my face.

As he slid his rod around, searching for ingress, I bit a clump of linens. Never had I imagined it would be like that.

The pain was nothing compared to the shame.

He was gentle, at first. But then, his breathing became labored, and it was as if a demon had taken hold of him. He clutched at my shoulders, grunting and rutting upon me like a mindless beast. His sweat was pungent and slick.

Then, abruptly, he gave a shudder and stopped. He uncoupled us and climbed off me to stand by the bed. His hands were on my thighs, and he was examining the space between.

"Well," he said. "It would seem you were a virgin. That is a relief."

◆

On April 14, 1873, the doctor lay the small bundle in my arms, and I swooned with happiness. It squirmed, as if delighted to be out of the confines of my body. Tiny pink feet, those that had kicked outward from inside, were free at last to kick at the great big world instead—and kick she did.

"What will you name her?" asked the doctor, peering down his hook nose from serious brown eyes.

"Rose," I said. "Rose Mary Poole. Rose was my mother's name. Mary was the name of Mr. Poole's mother."

"A solid choice," replied the doctor without a smile. "I'll make note of it then." He walked away, and I was drawn to gaze upon the pinched, splotched, gorgeous face of my daughter.

"Can my husband come in?" I asked.

The doctor opened the door. "Mr. Poole, your wife is asking for you."

"Is it over?" Orton asked.

"Yes, sir. Mother and daughter are fine."

"Daughter?"

I held my breath.

"Yes, sir. Your wife has informed me— "

A loud crash sounded in the hallway, and Orton hissed, "A girl!"

I heard him storm off, my heart rising higher in my throat with every thud of his boots. By the time the doctor returned, my face was hot and flushed with embarrassment.

The doctor averted his gaze. "I'll come back in the morning to check on you both." Then, he left.

Anna came in and sat beside me on the bed. I introduced her to her niece, and she beamed, as amazed by Rose as I was.

"You're happy," Anna said.

I smiled. "Kant said, 'Happiness is not an ideal of reason, but of imagination.' If that be the case, then I imagine I am indeed happier at this moment than I have ever been before."

We didn't speak again for a long time, content to listen to the musical sounds of a newborn; until finally, she asked, "Do you want me to talk to him?"

I knew she meant Orton. "No," I replied. "He doesn't make any secret of his feelings, never has. I'll just have to give him a boy next time."

"You do that," said Anna. "This baby is for you. He can have the next one."

We laughed, until she said, "But, I do think I need to give him a piece of my mind. He shouldn't treat you so."

"It's okay, dearest," I tried to reassure her. "I'm used to his moods. They don't affect me anymore."

"They affect me," said Anna with the same strength in her voice that had gotten us through the lean years after our parents had died.

◆

I slept on and off between feedings, and later, after the sun had gone down, Orton came to see me. He shuffled in with his hat in his hands and a tight smile on his face. His brown hair was wind-blown and damp.

"It appears," he said, "I owe you an apology." Tall and broad as he was, he made a strong presence at the foot of the bed.

"No," I said. "You don't."

"Your sister believes I do, and I've a mind to think she's right. It's not your fault."

I could hear him skirting around the words he was thinking but didn't want to say. It wasn't my fault I'd borne him a girl.

"She talked to you?"

"She gave me an earful of wasps." He came around the bed and bent to kiss me on the forehead. He smelled of night air, sweat, and pipe smoke. "Don't fret now. You rest. It's been a long day." He left, and I didn't need to be told twice. He had eased my mind about his unhappiness, and I was exhausted.

The next morning, the fog of sleep was slow to withdraw. I lay in bed, moving my legs, feeling the pain in my belly, and remembering the birth. I stretched, and a sudden prick of pain on my forearm caused me to cry out in alarm. I half sat up to see what had caused it.

There was a dead rose lying in the bed beside me, its stem brown and dry, its petals desiccated and crumbling. A petrified thorn had pricked me, and I found a smear of blood there.

I was certain it hadn't been there when I'd fallen asleep.

*Why,* I wondered, *would anyone do such a thing?*

Unnerved, I crawled out of bed, easing my way onto my feet. I ignored the pain and crept across the room to Rose's crib.

Ida, my maid, snuck in from the nursery a moment later. "Mrs. Poole, you shouldn't be on your feet yet. I can bring the baby to you." She had plain brown hair restrained in a bun at the nape of her neck. Wisps of it had escaped and curled around her crow's feet and the deep indents on either side of her mouth.

"I'm fine," I said. "I'd like to sit in the rocker and nurse her."

"Of course, ma'am." Ida hurried to pull the rocker closer and to put an extra cushion on the seat.

My baby was sound asleep, her skin already smoother, her little hands curled, and beside her, there was another dead rose.

"What is this?" I cried. "Ida, did you put this here?" I removed the crumbling flower from the crib and held it toward the nursemaid.

"No, ma'am," Ida said, fear in her eyes. "I'd never!"

There came a knock on the door, sober and steady.

I dropped the flower to the floor and picked up my child.

Ida hurried to the door. She opened it only a crack. "Yes?"

An unfamiliar voice, a man with dark edges around his tone, said, "Make your mistress presentable, madam. I would have a word with her."

Whoever he was, he had to wait in the hall for several minutes. By then, Rose was awake and hungry, and nothing else was ever so important. As I held her to my breast, I stopped wondering whether the dead flowers were threats or warnings, omens or mean-spirited commentary. My own perfect Rose drained me, and I knew a love more intense than ever before. Whispering near her bud of an ear, I promised I'd never let anything bad happen to her.

◆

The man at the door was a police officer, short and brawny, with eyes as black as the souls of the criminals he arrested. Upon first sight of him, I knew he hadn't liked waiting, but he entered and was as polite as he could manage. I had put on a dressing gown and was sitting in the rocking chair with Rose asleep in my arms.

Ida brought a chair forward, but the officer shook his head, choosing instead to stand in the middle of the room, shifting his weight from one foot to the other. "I have questions to ask you, Mrs. Poole," he said.

"What's this about?" I must have sounded like every other individual whose world was just about to crumble.

"When was the last time you saw your sister, Mrs. Poole?"

"Why, yesterday. She was here with me, just after the birth." A rancid unease collected at the bottom of my stomach.

"I see. And did she tell you what her plans were for yesterday evening?" He kept his hands clasped, as if afraid they would wander without tight control.

"I don't believe she had any. What's this all about? What's happened?"

The words rushed from him in a flurry. "I'm sorry to have to tell you this, but a fisherman found your sister this morning—dead—on the shore of the James. All her clothes were gone, and she had marks, most on her neck. Strangled, you see."

"What? No. You're mistaken. It can't be her.

She's in her room. It's too early for her to be up and about. Ida, come take Rose."

The officer shook his head, eyes tight with discomfort. "Your husband has confirmed it's her." He dug in one of his pockets.

"My husband?"

"Yes, ma'am. We found the lady's purse... had a letter addressed to this manor. We spoke with your husband first thing." From his pocket, he pulled a choker—a black ribbon with a cameo just like... "I was told I could return this to you." He held it out.

The choker lay heavy in my hand. It had suffered little damage.

"It was also in her purse, ma'am. I'm sorry for your loss. Ma'am?"

Ida took the baby.

A stubborn part of me didn't want to believe Anna was dead. I lurched down the hall to her room— her cold and silent room. Anna was gone. Suddenly, I knew it in my heart.

I don't remember anything between that moment and when I awoke in the dark, my head pounding.

For the briefest moment, I thought perhaps it had all been a bad dream, but then I heard voices coming from the nursery. They weren't *quite* whispering. It was Ida, and she said, "Poor young girl, beaten to death. Can you imagine? Right under our noses."

Another female voice replied, "And poor Mrs. Poole, losing her sister so soon after birthin' a young'un. Makes my heart ache."

"And Mr. Poole, leaving the job of telling her to a complete stranger... Terrible."

"Tsk. Poor Mrs. Poole."

I threw back the covers, went to the window, and gazed out at the dark river. The moon had just begun to rise, and it sat in the tops of the trees, enormous and hungry.

*How had this happened? Anna...how?*

A movement near the dogwood caught my eye, and I found myself being scrutinized by the Charred Lady. It was the same woman I'd seen the night before my wedding. Her face was ghoulish, her skull misshapen inside the cloak's hood. A flash of silver at her throat was the only thing that distinguished her from Death himself.

One moment she was there, and the next she was gone.

A burning smell filled the room, the unmistakable aroma of smoke and singed hair. I turned, my heart racing, fearing the house was on fire, but no... It was her.

She was there, in the room with me, and she

had brought the smells with her. She had been in a fire, and given the extent of the damage, I couldn't imagine how she had survived. In truth, I knew she hadn't. Her mouth and nostrils were blackened, and her one good eye bloodshot and swollen. Her skin had shrunk as if the padding underneath had melted, and she had no hair left, just ragged remnants with singed ends, ginger-colored tufts.

I stumbled away from her, my back coming to rest against the window frame, and my breathe came in small tight gasps, more like sobbing than respiration.

"Anna?"

There'd been no mention of her having been burned, perhaps in reverence to my sensibilities.

She raised an arm as if to point at the bed, though her fingers did not uncurl.

I looked where she indicated and saw a trail of dead roses leading into the nursery, a garden path left to seed.

"No!" I shouted, and the cork barricading my emotions popped free. I willed her gone with every ounce of my being, closed my eyes, and let all my fear and fury, my grief and confusion, flow out of me into a series of screams unlike any noise I'd ever made in my life.

Next thing I knew, I was surrounded—Ida and

the other maid, a houseboy, the butler—with hands and voices trying to get me under control. I fought them, and as my conscious mind resurfaced, a mother's instinct rose in me. My thoughts focused on getting to my daughter.

But they wouldn't allow it, and before I could convince them, the doctor arrived with a draught of laudanum. I was delivered unto oblivion.

◆

I attended the funeral as a ghost of myself, unaware of the faces passing before me, offering condolences. It was a closed casket, by Orton's order. When I ventured a query about this to the mortician, he told me it was for the best; she wouldn't have looked like herself.

I demanding to see her and when they refused, I screamed. When they couldn't get me to stop, they carried me from the church. The doctor came, with his serious eyes and more laudanum.

The next morning, they moved the crib and rocking chair out of my bedroom and into the nursery next door. I complained, but they said it was for my own good. I couldn't argue, not then. I didn't have the strength.

◆

"I'm concerned for my daughter, doctor," said Orton. I could hear him through the door. He was just outside my room in the hallway. I was lying in the bed where he'd first taken me, where he'd given me my Rose, and where I'd brought her into the world from my womb.

"My wife has been under a lot of strain, and she's always had a bad case of nerves. As much as I hate to say it, I think she needs more help than I can give her."

"I'll draw up the paperwork," replied the doctor. "Don't you worry, Mr. Poole. I know a young woman who has an infant of her own. She has more than enough milk for both. For now, I recommend you let your staff care for your wife. She'll need constant supervision to ensure she doesn't injure herself. I'll stop by again in a couple days."

"You don't think she'd hurt our child, do you, Doctor?"

"When it comes to the welfare of a child, one can never be too cautious. I've seen this kind of thing before. Women are driven by their emotions, Mr. Poole. No man can predict what they will do when hysterical. For now, I recommend you keep her away from the baby."

"Orton?" I called. I wanted to reassure him. I wanted to see—to nurse—my daughter.

Their footsteps moved on, or perhaps I was drifting away from them, into the darkness of my own mind.

I had no light inside me, nothing to illuminate my path, at first. But then the flickers came, like fireflies casting their teasing glimmers upon the details of a darkened shoreline. I saw bits and pieces come to light, portions of the truth, memories that gave me proper questions.

It was the middle of the night when I got out of bed and fumbled my way to the armoire. From inside it, I took a small trinket box and found the battered cameo. The moment it was in my hand, she was there with me. I smelled her before anything else, stronger than before; burning wood and flesh choked my sinuses and made me gag.

The laudanum in my blood gave me courage.

"You brought this to me, didn't you?" I asked, not expecting a reply. "You were trying to warn me. But how, Anna? You were still here with me."

She didn't move, just stared back at me with her one eye, so familiar, so like my own.

I said, "Who did this to you? You have to help me understand."

She stood still in the middle of my room, then

was gone. An instant later, she reappeared by the window, looking back at me. She gestured for me to follow her and again disappeared.

I was frozen for only a second before running to the window.

There she was, on the lawn, her cloak hanging heavy and still around her despite the wind bending the trees.

*Should I follow her?* I wondered. She wanted to show me something, maybe about her death. *Maybe she would lead me to her murderer.*

I put on my robe and my wool coat, slid my bare feet into riding boots, and crept down the back stairs. As I stepped out through the back door, she was waiting for me, on the lawn.

The Charred Lady didn't let me get close, but appeared and disappeared like a lighthouse, guiding me away from—I hoped—jagged rocks. She led and I followed, shivering in the darkness, wondering what she had to show me.

*Metaphysics,* Herr Kant had written, *is a dark ocean without shores or lighthouse, strewn with many a philosophic wreck.*

The night bugs were chirping with a regular rhythm, and a splash reminded me of the James River's proximity. She took me straight to the dock and its boathouse.

I'd never liked the boathouse. It gave me an uneasy feeling. It wasn't that I didn't trust the floorboards to hold me nor the fact it had no windows to let in light, nor the many strange spiders living in its dark corners. It was more how it crouched there, as if waiting, malevolent and leering.

The ghost appeared at the door and signaled me to go inside.

My skin crawled at the back of my neck and across my scalp. I nearly ran, back to the manor, but I reminded myself Anna would never allow any harm to come to me.

I lifted the latch on the door and pulled it open. The rusty hinges squealed as if in pain, and the smell of fish rushed out of the building. I felt around until I found the lantern and match box on the shelf just inside.

Once lit, the lantern cast a timid glow upon the boathouse's interior. It was stalled by the many tools, oars, and benches blocking it from getting into the corners.

The Charred Lady was standing in the far corner of the room, gazing down at her feet. She lifted her one good eye to me, then looked down again. I leaned to one side to see what she saw, but I was too far from it.

As if sensing my reluctance to approach her, she

disappeared. The smell of her left at the same time, and I breathed easier. I listened but heard nothing other than the sounds of crickets and frogs. I picked my way across the room to where she'd been standing.

Upon the floor, a rug, woven of ragged cotton, dirty and old, had one corner flipped up. I didn't understand, but there was nothing else she could have meant.

I lifted the corner with two fingers and found a trap door.

Beside it, caught between two floorboards was a china button, white with tiny blue flowers I recognized. It had belonged to Anna. My hand shook as I picked it out of the crack, my tears causing it to swirl out of focus. I held it to my bosom and sat down, there, on the spot where Anna must have died, in the dark, on this filthy wooden floor, with the smell of the river thick in her nostrils.

*Had she cried out? Had she fought back?*

The trap door wasn't locked, and I don't know what made me open it—a morbid desire for completion perhaps or the hope I'd find a clue. I pulled the trap door open and held the lantern aloft.

About five feet below was the river, lapping toward shore, splashing against the wooden posts. The boathouse was supported by pilings, out over the water. I assumed the trap door was for loading equipment into and out of boats.

I stayed there for a long time, staring at the black water that had carried my sister downstream.

"Anna!" I cried. But the Charred Lady didn't return.

When I went back to the manor, I sneaked inside, not wanting anyone to catch me out alone, late at night, in a dirty nightgown.

As I tip-toed by the library door, I saw Orton in there, at his desk. He had a whiskey glass at his elbow, its golden contents gleaming in the lamplight. His attention was intent upon papers spread before him. I hurried up the stairs to my room, eager to see my baby.

Rose was sleeping, plumper and creamier than ever. Ida was there too, on her cot, fast asleep as well. I picked up the child and took her to the rocking chair. I don't know how long I sat there with her, rocking, singing lullabies, and chasing thoughts of Anna from my mind.

◆

I awoke to screaming, the kind of high-pitched horrified squeal of a horse caught in a burning barn. It jolted me upright in bed, though it took me a moment to realize the screams were coming from the nursery. Before I knew I had moved, I was there, standing beside Ida, and she was backing away from me, bent at the waist as if someone had punched her in the stomach. I looked from her to the crib and saw my Rose—gray and stiff, dead.

Then, I was screaming too.

◆

The doctor came, and I welcomed the laudanum. I let it carry me away on its cloud. Time stretched and warped.

Weeks passed.

My husband came and went, rarely staying longer than it took me to notice him. I never saw Ida again, but there was a new girl who hovered near me, helping me with a body's needs. She said her name was Blanche, and she had a sweet voice that could also be commanding when necessary.

Days turned into nights, collecting in weeks and months.

Blanche's encouragements worked their way into my consciousness and coaxed me from my stupor. Gradually, thoughts emerged from the space between the numbness and the emotions, between the sobs and the emptiness.

"You're young, Mrs. Poole. I know it's no comfort now, but you've your whole life ahead of you. I know plenty of ladies who've lost a child and went on to have many more. You're not alone. Your husband's worried about you. You can get through this, ma'am. I know you can. Any woman's had a baby can do anything. God will send you another angel to care for." Sarah went on and on for hours until I almost started imagining she was right.

One day, I got out of bed.

The next, I took a bath.

The following, I went into the nursery to find it barren and cold. All of Rose's things were buried in trunks in the corner. Her crib was as empty as my soul. I didn't cry that day. I'd already cried myself dry.

The next day, I dressed and went downstairs with the intent of joining my husband for lunch. He was in the library with the black-eyed police officer. I didn't mean to eavesdrop, but I couldn't bring myself to turn away once I'd overheard the topic of their discourse.

Orton said, "She's under a doctor's care, officer."

"Mr. Poole, I need to see her soon. Forgive me for speaking bluntly, but there's still confusion about the cause of death. The coroner believes the infant was suffocated. She had...bruising, sir."

My heart fell all the way down into my belly.

"You don't," cried Orton, incredulous, "believe my wife could kill her own child?"

"We never like to think so, sir, but it does happen. Given the recent death of her sister, I imagine your wife must have been in a fragile state in recent weeks?"

I waited for Orton to defend me, to tell the police officer I would never harm my baby, never *ever*.

He said, "She's been acting erratically, but murder? She'd have to be insane. If that's her condition, then her doctor will know."

The officer sniffed. "All righty, sir. I'm sorry for your loss. If I were in your shoes, I don't know what I'd do. Bottom line, if your wife did it—and it appears she did—then she's either going to jail or to an asylum for the rest of her life. I need to speak with her soon. I can't put it off no longer. I'll be in touch, sir."

My legs went weak. I clung to the stair railing and dragged myself upward as quickly as I could. I didn't think he'd seen me, but I couldn't be sure. Appetite lost, I returned to the nursery and collapsed in the rocking chair.

*Had I?* I tried to remember if she'd been moving, if she'd been breathing, when I put her back in the crib. I'd held her that night, for a long time. I remembered her stirring in my arms, waking once or twice and suckling at my breast. I'd been awake the whole time, I was sure of it.

*Had I suffocated her—accidentally?*

The door to the nursery opened, and Orton stepped inside.

"Amelia?" he asked. "What are you doing in here? Why are you sitting in the dark?"

Darkness had fallen, and I hadn't noticed.

I remembered a tiny set of fingers wrapping around my grown one. I'd been laying her down in the crib, and she hadn't wanted me to go. I'd had to pry her fingers from mine. She'd been alive. My Rose had been alive when I left her.

"Orton," I said. "I didn't kill her."

"I know," he replied. "Come with me, Amelia." He came to me and helped me up from the rocker, then slid an arm around my waist and walked me out of the room.

"Where are we going?" I asked.

"Don't worry. I'm going to fix everything. I made a bad decision, and now I have to make it right." His mouth was thin and tight, his gaze directed forward as if he could see his destination and was willing himself there.

In the mud room, he pulled my emerald cloak off a hook and wrapped it around me, clasping the silver pin at the neck. I watched him as he pulled the hood up over my head.

He said, "Don't want you to catch cold now, do we?" Then, he walked me out the back door, onto the lawn.

"I'm in my slippers," I told him.

"It doesn't matter." He kept his arm around me, tight, controlling.

My slippers were getting wet; my feet were cold. A brisk wind blew inland off the river, carrying a chill. Orton walked us toward the boathouse.

"What are we doing?" I asked.

After a few steps, he repeated, "I need to show you something."

The boathouse loomed ahead of us, and I saw her, standing beside it, cast in shadow. It was the Charred Lady, watching us.

A wave of fear washed over me, and I balked.

"I don't want to go there," I said. "Not tonight." I tried to twist away, but his arm tightened around me, and he latched onto my wrist.

"Stop it," he commanded, his tone dropping into dark depths. "I can't take it anymore."

"You can't take what?"

"I didn't bargain for any of this. I married you, but instead of the perfect family, I got your smart-mouthed sister and a girl child to put me in the poor house. Why couldn't you have had a boy?"

"You're hurting me!" I tried to peel his crushing fingers off my wrist. He pulled me forward so harshly I fell to my knees in the grass.

"Lord have mercy." He hauled me to my feet.

When we got to the boathouse, he pulled open the door and shoved me inside. I stumbled a bit but caught myself with a hand on one of the wooden work benches.

"Orton, please!"

He picked up the lantern and the box of matches. "Dear, stupid Amelia," he said. "I know you feel guilty about the baby. You may even feel guilty about your sister. It *was* your fault, you know? You never should have told her to come at me. She provoked me. What kind of man would I be if I let a woman use that tone with me?"

Orton was silhouetted in the doorway. Behind him, I could see the house up the hill, lights shining in various windows.

"What are you saying?" I could barely gasp the words out.

"Biggest mistake of my life was marrying you. You've been nothing but trouble ever since the day we said our vows, and now I'm doomed to spend my life chained to a wife in an asylum. I deserve better."

Orton lit a long wooden match, and the flare licked across the contours of his face, deepening his eye sockets and making his jaw a hard line of pure evil.

"Maybe I didn't need to smother the child, but do you have any idea how expensive it is to raise a girl? The fancy party dresses, school expenses, dowry, and for what? What would she ever do for me? She'd go off and marry, and I'd get nothing. A boy could have been my business partner. I'd have guided him, molded him. We'd have been unstoppable." His voice grew dreamy for a moment, but then it changed, hardening. "Amelia Foster Poole, I hereby divorce you."

"It's not my fault!" I cried.

"Yes. You brought too many mouths into my house, to many useless mouths to feed."

Orton threw the unlit lantern to the boathouse floor as hard as he could. It cracked and spilled its oil. Then, he held the match to an old rag on the shelf. It ignited, flames blazing upward, and Orton pushed it off onto the floor.

"Help!" I screamed. "Help! Help me!"

Orton shook his head. "There's no one to hear you. I gave the staff the night off. Scream all you want."

I backed away, watching the fire race over the oil.

Orton walked out and slammed the boathouse

door shut.

The only light came from the spreading fire. It began to catch twigs, pinecones, and other flammables. Smoke rose thick and choking between me and the door. I wrapped the edge of my cloak over my nose and mouth.

The Charred Lady was there, on the other side of the flames, looking at me. The fire licked at her legs, and gray demon smoke curled about her head.

I was looking in a mirror, mesmerized by her, by the cloak exactly like my own.

She stared back at me as the flames engulfed her, and I understood. She wasn't Anna; she was me. I was my own ghost.

As the flames leapt, Herr Kant's metaphysical theories engulfed me. I saw numbers, calculations, and equations in the writhing shadows on the walls, and in a moment of enlightenment, I knew he'd had it right. *Time works however a person chooses to perceive it.* Imagination precedes Creation. I could imagine myself happy, imagine my spirit traveling through time to give a dire warning. I could imagine myself escaping, and...

I couldn't breathe. I had to get out. Coughing, I bent down and lifted the rug. The heat was unbearable, and a corner of my cloak was smoldering.

I pulled at the trap door, but it wouldn't budge.

The Charred Lady tipped her head back and began to scream.

It was stuck!

Desperate to escape, I got my legs under me and put both hands on the handle. I tugged with all my might.

The trap door lurched free, and I fell backward into stacked clay pots and garden tools. Dislodged objects—I didn't know what—dropped down on my head, and I shielded myself with my arms.

The flames climbed to the ceiling. It was so loud, the crackling, the roar—and the screaming.

I righted myself and crawled toward the hole, blinded by smoke and tears. My hand fell through the opening. I allowed the rest of my body to fall, head-first, into the river. The water crashed into me, then engulfed me.

For several moments, I was upside down and fighting the urge to cough while underwater, but then I felt the slick bottom. I got my feet under me and pushed my head to the surface.

Gasping and choking—the smoke still so thick—I had no idea which way to go to find safety, so I struck out blindly, pushing with my legs. The cloak was too heavy. I unclasped it and let it float away from my shoulders. The current claimed one of my slippers.

I half-walked, half-swam, distancing myself

from the boathouse. I was grateful for the river's cold embrace and the fresh air filling my lungs.

A loud crash signaled the boathouse's collapse. The Charred Lady had long since stopped screaming.

Trees on the shore, undergrowth, hid me when I crawled out of the river. I didn't want Orton to see me. I kept to the trees, slipping from shadow to shadow and made my way back toward the main house. As I neared, I spotted the flaring ember of his cheroot high up on the mansion's widow's walk. He was fiddling while Rome burned.

I skirted around the house, out of sight, and slipped in through the front door.

Kicking off my one remaining slipper, I hurried in my bare feet to the library. My dress was wet and heavy, hanging so low as to drag behind me on the floor and leave a smear of mud and water in my wake. I lifted the hem in the front to keep from tripping and rushed across to Orton's desk.

Shortly after our wedding, my husband had made a grand display of showing me where he kept his gun, how to load it, and how to fire it. I could still hear his voice, "Wife, I want you to know how to defend our home in case brigands show up while I'm away." I appreciated the irony as I loaded the revolver, and the act of putting the bullets in their little holes soothed me.

I ceased gasping for breath, ceased shivering.

Access to the widow's walk was at the back of the house, through the attic. On the way, I passed Anna's room and the nursery. My feet were silent.

The door to the attic was open. I climbed the stairs to the top of the stone manor. The walk itself was a wide platform with a railing around it. From there, a woman could watch for her man to come sailing home along the river.

Orton had his back to me as I stepped onto the widow's walk. The tip of his cheroot created a stream of red light as he moved his hand down to the railing, and the ice clinked in his whiskey glass. Beyond him, in the distance, I could see the orange glow of the fire. The boathouse had collapsed, and the dock still burned, visible against the black river.

A rustle of fabric, or the smell of smoke or river mud, made Orton turn. His eyes widened in surprise, for just a flash, then his whole face tightened.

"Amelia," he said. "You witless bitch. This could have been all over. Now, you're going to make me hurt you even more."

I looked him straight in the eyes. "There's nothing you can do to hurt me more than you already have, Orton. You stole my life. There's nothing left of me but a ghost." My hand didn't shake as I pointed the gun at him.

Orton took a long, thoughtful pull on his cheroot. "You don't have it in you."

I showed him what I had in me. I shot the walk at his feet.

He took a dancing step backward. "Hey!" The whiskey glass shattered where it landed.

"The next bullet goes in your leg, Orton." I lifted the muzzle.

"No!" he cried. "Wait! What are you doing?"

"I'm destroying the one thing you love best, husband. You." I fired and missed again, the bullet going out beyond him into the lawn. He stumbled backward, and his eyes darted as he searched for a path to escape.

"Next time," I said, "I can't miss. Bigger target." I aimed the gun at his gut.

"Amelia, no!" He threw his cheroot at me. It sparked a bit when it hit my skirts, but I was too wet.

Orton tried to rush past me, and I put the barrel of the gun right in his face. He dodged and leapt over the railing.

I hurried to look.

He'd landed about ten feet below on the slanted roof and was sliding down it, slowing his descent with hands and feet. Gravity had hold of him, and the roof didn't give him much traction. The lower half of his body slid off.

I aimed again, and he saw me do it.

Panicking, scrambling to get away, he dropped over the roof's edge, hanging on with his hands. Except he moved too quickly, as he always had. For a moment, it looked like he might catch himself, but then his own weight dragged him free of the fragile hold he'd acquired. He didn't have the strength.

And I didn't have to waste another bullet.

He screamed as he fell...and the sound ended abruptly when he hit the stone patio below.

Herr Kant once wrote: *If man makes himself a worm, he must not complain when he is trodden on.*

◆

It wasn't difficult to play the grieving widow. I had more than enough grief to fill my eyes and heart. The coroner determined Orton's death was an accident. He said Orton must have seen me down by the boathouse, trying to put out the fire, and in a moment of grave worry, he leaned too far out over the railing and fell. It was a terrible tragedy.

Of course, it would have been a shock if the coroner had actually managed to get it right that time.

After the police left, I returned to my room, exhausted. The only thing left on my mind was sleep. But, as I slid under the covers, I felt something in the bed: a book. I turned up the lamp so I could examine it.

It was a copy of Kant's *What is Enlightenment?* I opened the book to the first page and discovered my final communication with the Charred Lady, a portion of the text underscored. I read: *'Have the courage to use your own intelligence!' is therefore the motto of enlightenment.*

A violent shiver went up my back. I had stared into the terrible face of my own fate, one of them, and she, the alternate me, had gone beyond time to help me avoid her terrible end.

Time had proven fluid, and I had noticed.

Inspired, despite my fatigue, I stayed up into the dim hours of morning, putting my thoughts to paper. The last thing I penned that night, though I'd write much more in the years to come, was:

*My life has burned to the ground. The other Mrs. Poole died in the boathouse, and now I am just Amelia, not a sister, not a wife, not a mother, and not a ghost. Sapere aude. Dare to know.*

# Cookies for Gio

I rest a hand on Gio's shoulder, and he looks up from the half-naked pop star writhing on his computer monitor, a smile lingering on his face. That's my hormonal eighteen-year-old. My heart aches on its next beat.

"Hi, Mom," he says, head loose on his neck. He wrangles it under control and pushes his headphones off one ear.

"Hi." I sit on the bed, within reach of him in his electric wheelchair, and I pet its vinyl-covered arm-rest. Gio doesn't need it all the time. His Muscular Dystrophy hasn't progressed that far. On his good days, he shuffles around with a walker.

I ask, "Whatcha doin'?"

"Soaking up as much Internet as I can," Gio says, his tongue thick, words carefully pronounced. "Before they take it all away. What are...you doing?" He sets his hand on mine. His fingers are cold, soft, and awkward. I hold them, warm them, love them.

"Just taking a break from the computer."

He leans toward me, eyes bright with interest. "Hacking?"

"Shhh." I look over my shoulder, then feel ridiculous—and yet...

He whispers, "You think they're listening?"

I shrug. "I'm baking cookies. Got it?"

Gio tips his head back and chortles. "Got it!" I feel the weak squeeze of his hand in mine. "I love your cookies."

"You hungry?"

"No. When's Dad going to call?"

"Truth?"

"Always."

"I don't know." It's been nine months since Antonio was drafted, and forty-five days since we last talked to him. A portion of his paycheck appears every month, so I know he's alive. Last time I spoke to him, he said something about being transferred to the Templar brigade. He said they might send him to fight in Jordan.

I release Gio's hand and pretend to watch the video with him, following his cues to laugh, hiding the worries that are surging over me. What if I get caught in the deep underground? How will we pay for Gio's care? What if Antonio is killed in Babylon?

They're calling the war "The Final Crusade." The American attack on Israel and Palestine surprised everyone. They surrendered without a whimper, and U.S. forces installed a provisionary government. The evangelists proclaimed a victory for Jesus.

War correspondents showed gleeful American soldiers swimming in the Sea of Galilee. The media crows about battles won, enemies thwarted, and territory gained in Cyprus, Lebanon, and Syria. Damascus broke months ago, and Jordan is on its way to surrender.

The president's press secretary keeps saying, "The president is taking whatever measures are necessary. America has had enough. We tried the olive branch. It didn't work, so now we use the stick. It's time someone lifted Muslims out of their semi-barbarous state. Children under ten will be given new names, new families, and new lives. They will be raised with God's love. All the rest are criminals. Either you're with us, or you're against us."

Gio cries out, jerking me alert. He's pointing a shaky hand at the screen.

"What's the matter?" I ask. I realize my back has hunched under the weight of my thoughts, and I sit up straight.

"Look." Gio unplugs his headphones, and the sound breaks out into the room.

Propaganda. A camera-shot of the Oval Office is zooming in toward the desk where the president of these United States is signing a bill into law.

The narrator says, "In the wake of the Secretary of State's amendment to the Immigration and Nationality Act which added Hebrew groups to the list of Domestic Terrorist Organizations, the president has today signed an executive order requiring the seizure of all assets held by these groups. Warrants are being served to hamstring those who would attack us from within. A hundred and twenty Jewish leaders and rabbis are en route to Guantanamo."

I have friends who are Jewish. Or, I had friends. I haven't heard from them since the Israel invasion.

The music video comes back on, in media res, and I stand up. I don't want Gio to see me cry.

"I better get back to those cookies," I say, heading for the door.

"Go get 'em, Mom."

◆

I go fishing for Jedi_Jock. I've known him since I was a student at M.I.T., though I have no idea where he is, what he looks like, or even if he's truly a man. I don't care. He's the most reliable human being on this planet, from my point of view.

I create a private chat room called Black-Wall2019, and I type: *Knock, knock, Jackass.* That's our code. His bots will find it. Now I just have to wait until he shows.

SnubNoseCock wants in... Nope, not him.

PwnYrPolitics... No.

ScissorSix66... Reject.

The deep underground is buzzing about the fall of Iran under Soviet expansion. "America's #1 ally," is the second prong in the war on everything non-Christian. Political cartoonists are calling the two countries the two-headed bear.

There. JJPussyGrabber... That's him. His public alias. I let him in, but wait for him to type first. He does: *Hey. What are you wearing?*

*My Trump-for-President pajamas. Flannel. You?*

*A clown suit.*

It's definitely him. I type, *We're secure.*

*Been awhile. How's the pet?*

*Good and bad. You know.*

I told him about Gio when Antonio got drafted, breaking the first rule of underground engagement, but I couldn't help it. I was at the end of my rope, alone, and I needed someone to talk to. So JJ knows I have a kid with M.D., but that's all he knows.

*Cool. They done?*

He's talking about the malware I'm programming, the virus meant to burn down firewalls all over the world. It'll free the 'Net, if only for a little while, and it's been one of the hardest tasks I've ever undertaken.

*Yes. All done.*

*K. Sit tight. We're planning a party for any time now. I'll get back to you.*

*You sure about this?*

*Having doubts?*

*I dunno. Maybe. It's just so...* (I almost type "extreme," but it's one of the words on Homeland Security's watchlist.) *...big.*

JJ types, *I wish you could see what I see. It's worth it.*

I feel sick. I'm a programmer, not a rebel. I've always stayed within the law.

I type, *OK*

*TTYL.* And, he's gone.

There's a flash on my monitor. My heart skips a beat. In a panic, I shut it all down and sit there, waiting for the sky to fall, the door to explode inward, and the uzi-toting black ops to close in. I wait all night, sleep like crap, and wake up in the morning feeling head-achy. Exhausted, but not arrested.

I fix Gio's breakfast around nine. I have to remind him to eat. He's never hungry anymore. It's the M.D. If I weren't here, he'd starve.

He's sitting at his computer, like always, typing

with frantic deliberation. Focused.

"Mother fucker!" he shouts before he realizes I'm there. I pause in the doorway, watching the images on his screen. It's another anti-gay ad from the series. Gio's mad, but not at the ad. Those are nothing new, not anymore.

Gio has a chat window open, though I can't read what's being said.

"Hey, buddy," I say. "It's time to eat." I move to stand beside him.

"Okay," he replies, distracted, sparing me only a glance. "Leave it there. I'll eat it."

"What's going on? You seem upset."

"I think they shut down Changyin. Her email's bouncing, and Twitter says her account is dead. Mark thinks they're deporting her."

"Oh, honey, I'm sorry." Changyin lived next door to us, back when we could afford a house in the suburbs. Her parents immigrated from China during the dot-com surge. Changyin was born here, in America. She's never known any other home.

"It's not right!" Gio's body shakes. "We have to do something!"

"She'll be okay," I say, lying through my teeth. "She's with her parents."

"There's only her mom and her sister," he says, voice as heavy as funeral bells. "Her dad died in the

Ammon siege, fighting for America."

I fiddle with the plate and silverware on the tray, straightening them. "It's time for breakfast."

"Mom...," Gio says, tentative. "The kids at my school are organizing a protest."

As the words unfold in my mind, I'm already shaking my head.

"Just listen, Mom." He turns his chair to face me and looks me square in the eyes, expression earnest. "All this stuff they feed us is bullshit. They're lying to us. For all I know, they're taking people out and shooting them."

"They wouldn't do that," I say, but I don't know that. You hear things in the underground that contradict the images shown on television.

Gio hits himself in the forehead with both hands. "Our world is shrinking. We watch what they want us to watch, do what they want us to do."

"I know. But there's nothing we can change about that." I place my hand on his bony shoulder. "You could get hurt. And for what? We can't stop what's happening. We can't save Changyin."

Gio waves his hands in the air, an awkward imitation of his father's Italian gestures. "We can't sit here and do nothing! If we do, then we're no better than they are." He leans forward, shaking like a baby bird whose head is too heavy. "We have to use our voices. They can't take those away!"

His breathing has grown strained.

I say, "I'll think about it, okay?" I set the tray on the desk, pushing his keyboard aside. "Do you want some help eating?"

"You promise you'll think about it? It's really important to me, Mom."

"I'll think about it. When is it?"

"Today, at noon, at the school."

"I'll think about it. You need help?"

"No, I got it."

"Okay." I hesitate, watching as he struggles to pick up his spoon. But ultimately, I leave. He deserves his dignity.

◆

JJPussyGrabber sends me an e-vite to a child's birthday party for the following evening. I R.S.V.P. that I'll be there. I don't know what the plan is or who else is involved. I know that my job is to release my malware. It's ready, waiting in its electronic Petri dish to be unleashed on the world. Desperate times call for desperate measures, someone once said. I doubt their times were as desperate as ours.

At 10:30, Gio starts moving around his room. "Mom! We have to catch the bus in half an hour."

I have no idea whether I'll let him go or not, or how I'll stop him if he insists. He's eighteen. Old enough to make his own choices. Though his body is weak, his mind is sharp. He's my brilliant raggedy boy, becoming a man. His heart may not be strong, but his Heart, capital H, is.

I'm not good at saying "no" to him. Will I have to physically bar him from leaving? Can I bring myself to do that? Am I overreacting? They're high-school kids. In another world, at another time, I'd have applauded this as a healthy Civics lesson. Has our world changed so much?

"Mom! We need to get going."

He rolls into the tiny living room with that look on his face, the stubborn one, and I know I'm in for a fight if I choose it.

"Gio, are you sure you want to do this?"

"Yeah, come on." He goes to the front door. "It'll be okay."

I'm so tired, I give in. "All right, but we're only staying for an hour, and we're sticking to the sidelines. Got it?"

"Sure. Let's go!" He's opening the door, and I have to chase him out into the hall with his coat.

◆

Many of the students are there when we arrive in the school parking lot. A bunch of them swarm Gio, hugging him and patting him.

Gio keeps asking, "Have you see Changyin? Is she here?"

A girl in a cheerleader outfit tells him, "She's gone, G. Her front door's got a USCIS memo about how we should stay out of the house and report any foreign nationals we know about. It's fucking insane." She looks up at me. "Sorry, Mrs. Esposito, but it is."

I just nod.

"Gee-man," says a kid I don't recognize. "Glad you could make it." He picks up one of Gio's hands and winds his own into. They shake, then bump knuckles as if they've done it a thousand times. It always unnerves me when I'm reminded that Gio has a life beyond our little hovel.

A beat later, Gio says, "You too, Mark."

"Look at this crowd, will ya? Damn. I never thought we'd get this many."

At the far end of the parking lot, kids begin to chant. "I am you and you are me! We deny your white supremacy!"

Gio moves his chair toward the edge of the crowd.

"Gio," I warn.

"This is sidelines, Mom. It's okay."

I look at the kids, their earnest faces, their lack of fear, and I feel just how brittle I've become.

The chant changes, "Say it loud! Say it clear! Immigrants are welcome here!"

More bodies press in behind us, more voices, all raised in concert.

I'm filled with pride, and much to my own surprise, I join the chant. Quiet at first, "Immigrants are welcome here." Then louder. "Immigrants are welcome here!"

The chant changes like a wave washing over the crowd. I hear the new one before it hits us, "Compassion is our passion!" It takes no time at all before the people around me, and I, are singing it out with force. I'm emboldened by my emotions.

One voice cuts through all the others, silencing me. It's loud enough that it makes the chant falter.

"Cease and desist! You are in violation of the Public Gatherings Act!" It's a man's voice, authoritative, belted out through a speaker.

The crowd resumes its chant. "Compassion is our passion! Compassion is our passion!"

"This is your second warning. Stop and go home, or face the consequences. You are breaking the law!"

The faces around me look defiant and determined, though some of the kids have the wherewithal to be scared. Gio, in his chair, is unperturbed.

I look around, searching for an avenue out, but the crowd filled in behind us.

"This is your last warning, people! Disperse! Go home!"

I begin to pull Gio's wheelchair backwards, forcing my way between bodies. He's just realized what I'm doing, and I haven't gotten very far, when a gunshot makes everyone jump and cringe.

The chant is interrupted again.

"Get down on the ground. I warned you. Get down on the ground, or we will use force!"

All around me, I hear, "Get down! Get down!" The crowd is complying.

I see the militiamen all around us.

The crowd drops in sections. They whisper their questions:

"Are they going to arrest us?"

"Did they shoot someone?"

"What are they doing?"

I drop to the ground with the others and reach up to pull Gio down with me, but the angle isn't right.

"Get down on the ground!" shouts the soldier.

"Gio!" I cry. "Get down here."

But Gio isn't listening. He's staring straight ahead, expression hard as a rock.

"Gio!" I grab his pant-leg and pull one of his feet off a stirrup.

He looks down at me then, and our eyes meet. His face is set. I've never seen it like that.

"Mom. I have to make my stand now, while I still can."

With a monumental effort, he pushes himself up out of his wheelchair.

I don't know why, but I let him. I watch, frozen, hypnotized by his bravery and by the surreal impossibility of the situation. I watch as he gains control of his balance and raises his chin.

He shouts, "Right takes might! Don't give up the fight!"

I see, everyone sees, that he has wet his pants.

"Right takes might!" he cries. "Don't give up the fight!" His voice rings out into history, across the crowd, and is forever etched in my memory.

As is the sound of the second gunshot and the crumple of his body back into his chair.

For one eternal moment, no one breathes. I can't believe...

Then, I'm moving. I crawl up and over him, protecting him from all else that might come. I smell his blood.

"Gio!" I cry. "Gio, no!"

The crowd is silent. Time has stopped.

One shout kicks it forward. "Right takes might!" It's the voice of a girl. "Don't give up the fight!"

Then the crowd is surging upward. Gunshots are ringing out like firecrackers. Screams are echoing off the high school.

Shaking, sobbing, I cling to my Gio, my brave raggedy boy, and I send my wail straight to God.

◆

They took him and all the others away in body bags. One kind soul guided me out of the chaos. He helped me onto the bus and off again at the right stop. He walked me inside and stayed until I fell asleep.

When I woke, he was gone. The apartment was silent but for the sirens outside.

The anonymous man—I don't even remember his face—had left a contraband digital camera and a note that said, "Do with this what you will."

It took everything I had to look at the footage.

I'm now sitting at my desk. The birthday party is about to begin, and I have cookies. So many cookies. Everything's ready, primed. I watch the clock, each passing minute like a lifetime.

When the time comes at last, I whisper, "This is for you, Gio." And I hit "enter".

My malware streaks out across the web, unblocking it, breaking open the channels of communication. And the first thing everyone will see is what they did to my Gio, and how one courageous young man stood up.

I crawl back onto the couch and curl into a ball. I think, "Right takes might. Checkmate, you dumb mother-fuckers."

———◆◆◆———

From the Wyrdwood Historical Society

# Nurse Magdaleine

*Hail Holy Queen, Mother of Mercy, our Life,*
*our Sweetness, and our Hope.*
*To thee, we cry, poor banished children of Eve.*
*To thee we send up our sighs, mourning,*
*and weeping in this vale of tears.*
— Catholic Rosary Prayer

The barrier between Earth and Gehenna is lifting. I feel it grow thinner with each passing moment. The sun is disappearing beyond the Atlantic; darkness descends, and spirits walk among the living. I see them. They look much as they did when they died, shriveled with illness or bloodied, skin the gray of death, jaundiced eyes hollowed by misery.

In the convent, I had time for reflection, and this I know: life is the process of dying. From the moment we're born, Death walks beside us. It haunts us with loving dedication, unwilling to let us forget—for long—that we belong to it. If this Great War has taught me anything, it's that no one escapes Death or the Judgment that follows—not Evil and not the sainted.

Yesterday, on La Toussaint, we venerated the saints, the martyred hallows, and all who have achieved the sanctity of le Paradis. My prayers to them echo in my heart, and I am replete with hope that, when it is my time, I will join them. I have lived a good life, one of which I am proud. I do not pretend to be worthy of sainthood, however, for I certainly am not.

Besides, today is not for the sainted. It is for the dead, les morts. Today is le Jour des Morts—02 Novembre. Souls held in Gehenna return to look upon the world they lost. No punishment was ever so painful as seeing how life continues after you're gone. The truth of one's own insignificance is humbling to those souls ready for absolution, and it is torture to those who are not.

From sunset to sunrise, the visiting spirits crowd around the living. They push and shove, jostling for position so they can whisper questions, curses, or endearments to the people they knew in life, as if they could still touch or even influence them somehow.

I've dreaded this return to Brest, but I came to see my friend and mentor, Doctor Benoît Beaulieu. My destination is the military camp where I used to work. I was a nurse, tending soldiers' bodies and minds, and thus, it is here that Doctor Benoît will look for me. I know this because I've seen him twice—always on 02 Novembre, le Jour des Morts—since we were separated by Death.

I enter through the gates, unchallenged; all are welcome on the Night of All Souls.

Some call this military installation "Pontanezen Camp," some "Camp Napoleon," and others "the rest camp." It's anything but restful. Everyone leaves here in only one of two ways: either with rifle to shoulder, headed toward the front, or with rifle emptied, headed toward the grave.

The camp has not changed, except that the smells of latrine, wood smoke, and truck exhaust hover thicker than I remember. There are no vibrant colors in the places of war, perhaps the rains—or the tears—wash them away.

The stone buildings resemble long coffins, set out in well-dressed rows, uniform. A haze obscures the farthest ones, fog rolling in from the harbor, the Rade de Brest. I'm used to this. This close to the cold ocean, the clouds are iron gray and heavy. A constant drizzle keeps the ground muddy and wool uniforms moist. The whole time I worked here, I never felt dry. I could never get warm. It's a sensation that has stayed with me, as if the cold took up residence in my bones.

Here is a drab American, half-obscured by the

waning light, forcing his shovel into the dirt with a stomp. His boot slips in the mud, and he nearly falls. He takes the Lord's name in vain. As soon as I look at him, I see how and when his life ends, as that is my gift and my curse.

*Balle, 5 Novembre, 1918.*

A bullet, three days hence. I make the sign of the cross and say a prayer that his passing happens quickly. I wish I could go back to the days when I didn't understand what I was seeing, when I didn't know so intimately the fragility of life. Ah, to be innocent again. I think back to my childhood in Landré-varzec, gathering eggs from the hens and milking the cow, my dog Pierrot at my heels. But then, my father was struck by a runaway carriage. I was sixteen.

Immediately after his death, I held a vigil for three days and three nights. I prayed, neither sleeping nor eating. I could not comprehend his loss. In my sorrow, I begged the saints to give me a reason, to explain why my father had been taken from me without warning. It was then that Saint Michel appeared to me. I could not look upon his saintly face for it was too beauteous, but I heard his words.

He said, "From this day forward, you will know the fates of men. You will renounce all that you hold dear, and you will be an instrument of peace among the dying. If you do this, you will one day take a seat beside our Father's throne."

It was as he said. From that day forward, I knew the timing and instrument of people's deaths, and when I looked in the mirror, I saw my own.

I foresaw when my mother would die, my friends, and everyone who attended church. I had much to learn about how to use my gift. If only I'd kept it to myself and never told anyone...

In that first week, I saw a man I'd known my whole life, Chrétian Dubolan.

*Couteau, 25 Fevrier, 1912.* That very evening, he was slated to die with a knife wound. I went to him, and I warned him. The look on his face, at first amused, then annoyed, should have discouraged me, but I didn't give up. I followed him and begged him to be careful. Eventually, he shoved me away.

He was the first, the first to come true. He died on the road, stabbed by a highwayman, and I learned that his death was God's business, not mine. I could not interfere, should not interfere.

The next day, word had spread throughout the village of his death and of my warning to him.

Everything changed then.

"Witch!" the citizens of Landrévarzec cried, throwing rocks and spitting on me. They refused me entrance to their shops, dragged their children inside, and closed their doors as I passed their homes.

"Demon child," the priest announced, crossing himself as if to ward me off.

My mother would not stop crying.

I had no other choice: I ran from my home in the night and traveled south along the main road, begging rides until I came to la Ville de Quimper. The Cathedral de Saint-Corentin reached into the heavens as if it bridged the gap between sinners and God, and I threw myself upon the mercy of the monks there.

That's when I first met Doctor Benoît and saw his death.

*La Grippe, 02 Novembre, 1918.*

I was dirty and hungry, my feet bloodied, and I had run like a coward from my calling to avoid persecution. I deserved no succor, but Doctor Benoît did not judge me. He cared not that I revealed neither my full name nor my full story, but took me to my new home with the Augustinian sisters of the Miséricord de Jesus and helped me to choose a new name, Magdaleine-Éloise. He convinced me I had suffered enough. To this day, I remember the kindness in his eyes and the feel of his hand. Weighty upon my shoulder, his touch anchored me in safety.

On the eve of taking my vows, I confessed my gift to Doctor Benoît. He did not treat me as if I were a liar, a madwoman, nor a cursed demon.

"Sister. I don't know what happened to you before you came here, however I do know that you have a kind heart. I agree with Saint Michel that you can be a great comfort to the dying."

"But how?"

He considered my question, then a wave of relaxation washed over him. He smiled. "As a nurse. Can you see it? I can."

I could, and I acted upon it immediately. During my training at the Hôpital-Géneral de Saint Antoine in Quimper, I worked closely with Doctor Benoît, and I learned to use my gift, my knowledge of Death's calendar, to ease the suffering of the dying. I became a nurse so I would be close to them—and to him.

Doctor Benoît and I arrived the first time at Pontanezen Camp in 1915 to work at the military hospital. Truck after truck was delivering soldiers from the front lines in pieces. We did our best to keep them alive and make them whole again. In a place rampant with death and fear, Doctor Benoît was my sanctuary.

During the day, we were a whirlwind in the camp hospital: triaging, treating, bandaging, and performing surgery. In the evenings, we went round to all our patients, together, and we prayed with them, laughed with them, cried with them, and encouraged them.

"Our suffering is finite," Doctor Benoît liked to say. "One day, it will end."

There's a French officer here. *Opium, 29 Jan-*

*vier, 1920.* He is herding soldiers toward the dining hall. "Fall in line!" he shouts, and they do as commanded.

On the interior, the stone barracks are divided into large rooms, some holding as many as a hundred beds, spaced with precision from wall to wall. This first one houses new soldiers, British and American, who have just disembarked from the enormous ships docked in Brest harbor.

As it's le Jour des Morts, there are spirits roaming between the cots, searching for familiar faces. Doctor Benoît will not be here. He'll be at the cemetery, beyond the hospital buildings. He knows to look for me there. But, I'm in no hurry. Tonight, I want to savor my memories. If all goes as I expect, this will be my last opportunity.

The façade looms over me as I move on. Soldiers stand in the shelter of the overhanging roof, in small groups, enduring the cold rain to smoke cigarettes and talk. I look at their faces, learn their deaths.

A gaunt American with two large front teeth says, "I heard the Fritzies got a big gun...can shoot a hundred kilometers, all the way to Paris from the front."

*Bombe, 6 Novembre, 1918.*

Further along, a British soldier with deep-set eyes the color of periwinkle says, "Bloody Hell.

They're dug in at Reims. Only way Alleyman's going to win this war is if they roust those Frenchies. I'm rooting for Jacques, but I wouldn't bet a shilling on it."

*Baïonnette, 4 Novembre, 1918.*

I watch a rugged young man drive his hand back through his curly brown hair. "I hail from the great state of Illinois. Name's Martin. Dang if I ain't happy to be off that boat."

*Balle, 5 Novembre, 1918.*

A Scotsman with a wide face and worry lines in his forehead, cigarette bobbing on his lip as he talks, says, "Aye. See this picture? Alice be the one on the right, and that other one's Moira. Pretty, don't you think? Alice is mine, but I'll introduce you to Moira when we get back."

*Balle, 6 Novembre, 1918.*

Death doesn't like to travel alone. Pauvre jeune-hommes. They are already like ghosts to me.

I pray, "Saint Michel, blessed is your name. By the power of God, defend these innocent souls in battle. Stand between them and the grip of the Devil. This I humbly beseech. Amen."

I don't want to know when and how they will die. I never have. It's God's business. But it was also His will that I be given this gift, so I do what good I can with it.

Unlike the living, the spirits of the dead do not trouble me. Once they've died, I no longer know how they met their ends, so I carry no burden for them. And yet, there are so many here, all in uniform of one kind or other: soldiers, nurses, doctors, Red Cross, all dead in this war, in the hospital beds in this camp, and buried beyond the wall in the cemetery.

One of the spirits stands taller than the rest. Ancient, his skin is fish-belly white, his auburn hair stringy, face hawkish, clothes ragged like kelp. Reddened eyes stare back at me as if he can hold me in place with them. He's one of the guards from Gehenna. A Fomorien. One of a demon-like race risen from the ocean to work at Death's door. Where there is one, there will be others.

The Fomorien takes a step toward me, and the sea of spirits parts like water before the bow of a ship as he continues forward, coming this way. The Fomoriens don't like me. They sense that I'm not normal and never was, that I walk the edge between life and death. I don't what they would do to me or how they would use me if they got their hands on me.

Run! I slip between the buildings, into the swarming crowd of dead—so many restless souls—toward the living. I'll be safe there, if I hurry.

I round a corner, stop, and look back to see if the Fomorien is still following. My nerves...

But, he's gone. Nowhere to be seen.

Then a voice—a woman's whisper nearby—draws my attention. "We lost another dozen overnight. I'm at a loss. That's over three hundred dead and another two-fifty sick. It's hopeless." Nurse Marcelle Roux has changed since the last time I visited. Her eyes have sunken deeper, as have her cheeks.

*Coeur, 12 Juillet, 1926.* I've always known that she would survive the war only to be done in by her heart.

"It's not hopeless," says the nurse with Marcelle. *La Grippe, 24 Decembre, 1918.* "Don't say that. They're looking for a cure. At least we haven't fallen ill yet." Yet. The influenza will take her by Christmas.

Marcelle and the other nurse walk toward the far end of the complex, keeping to the wooden planks placed down to form a path over the mud. The hospital buildings are that way. I follow.

Beyond where I can see, lies the cemetery, and more spirits emerge from the mists that shield it from view. More Fomoriens too. Unlike the timid or eager dead, the Fomoriens move with measured authority and strength. Le Jours des Morts is the one day a year when spirits are allowed leave from Gehenna, but their guards do not let them stray far. Nor are they allowed to interfere with the living.

Head down, walking with the two nurses, I go

into the first hospital building, to stay out of sight before I continue on to the cemetery where Doctor Benoît will be waiting for me.

Darkness and the chill of late Autumn permeate the camp hospital. The beds are all occupied. So many injured...and even more sick. They're congested and feverish. Blood collects at the corners of their mouths and in their nostrils. Vomit buckets sit between beds. The smell of sick hangs in the air, thick with the promise of infection.

*La Grippe, 2 Novembre, 1918*

*La Grippe, 4 Novembre, 1918*

*La Grippe, 7 Novembre, 1918*

*La Grippe, 10 Novembre, 1918*

*La Grippe, 10 Novembre, 1918*

*La Grippe, 15 Decembre, 1918*

*La Grippe, 22 Janvier, 1918*

I close my eyes.

"Purulent Bronchitis." Two doctors wearing surgical masks are discussing the disease in hushed tones. One is British, the other French. I move closer to better hear them.

"I've lost half my staff," says the French one, his face twisted with sorrow.

"I know. I'm not supposed to talk about it, but a colleague of mine working at Fillievres wrote to tell me that they're putting the infected in quarantine and leaving them to fend for themselves. They're evacuating the uninfected. I fear we must do the same. Sending these men out into the battlefield while they're contagious is unconscionable."

"Oui. It's spreading. The numbers I'm hearing add up to tens of thousands of dead already, here and in America."

"Bloody Hell. It's a pandemic. If this influenza continues to spread..."

I cross myself. Influenza. La Grippe. I know from experience how deadly it can be, and how quickly it spreads, especially between soldiers living in cramped quarters, sharing primitive latrines, and eating all together. I wish I could help them, but I gave up being a nurse on that fateful day in April, 1916.

I'll just go straight to the cemetery and wait there for Doctor Benoît, away from the sick and dying. The building's back door opens onto a road that will take me to the field where they bury the dead.

A dozen bodies on stretchers, covered with sheets, await burial. Their spirits linger nearby. One, a Frenchman who can be no older than eighteen, sobs. He understands what has happened. The others wander, confused, unwilling to stray too far from their bodies.

There's nothing I can do for them now. In many

ways, I am just like them, lost and alone, overcast by my sorrow, and desperate to see my dear friend again.

The old traditions still hold sway here. An older nurse is setting candles in jars along the road to guide the dead. Others are heading toward the cemetery with flowers and food, offerings for the departed.

I follow them to a large mound of dirt. There's a priest there, praying and waving a smoking censer.

"Dieu bénit Noé et ses fils, et leur dit: Soyez féconds, multipliez, et remplissez la terre. Vous serez un sujet de crainte et d'effroi pour tout animal de la terre..."

Go forth and multiply. The covenant with Noah. It continues, "And for your lifeblood, I will surely demand an accounting... I will demand an accounting for the life of another human being."

A nurse has fallen to her knees in the mud, her face twisted with sorrow, a crucifix held to her lips. Her white apron is splattered and stained.

"Forgive us," she prays.

Another kneels beside her, comforting her. "Shhh," she says. "We had no choice. There were too many. We had to."

Had to what?

Tokens lie upon the mound, mementos of lives that have ended. Cigarettes and liquor bottles left as gifts for the departed. Flowers and food. I comprehend. It's a mass grave. By the looks of the spirits, I conclude that they all died of influenza, their bodies buried quickly to keep the disease from spreading.

The spirits of those buried in the mound are unsteady. Moving like sheep, all as one, but undirected, with no destination in mind, they pull at their hair and clothes, eyes bulging with fear. One bleats, and they all take up the call, awakened from their stupor, roused by the noise. Like wolves howling at the moon, they cry out. So many. Too loud. Too pained!

The stoic Fomoriens walk among them as if taking an accounting of their number or state. Occasionally, one touches a spirit and says something I cannot hear. The spirit calms abruptly and replies as if asked a question. They then fall in line behind the Fomorien, no longer undirected.

Doctor Benoît is a good Breton, but his ancestors came from the isles. He heard the old tales, passed down from father to son for millennia. The Fomoriens, he once told me, are an ancient ruling people who come from Noah, beni de Dieu. Their magic made them the enemies of the fae, who were jealous of their God-given abilities—like mine. Doctor Benoît told me these things to reassure me that I was special, not strange, not cursed.

I angle away from the Fomoriens. The grave I seek is at the back of the cemetery.

A sober-faced soldier pulls a box of cookies
from his pocket and places them on a flat stone. *Foie,
10 Février, 1931.* This one at least will die neither in
a trench nor in the hospital here. Liver disease will
eventually drag him down.

With reverence, a man in a doctor's coat props
an old photo against a flower vase. His sorrow shows
on his face, and then he coughs violently. *La Grippe,
16 Novembre, 1918.*

I weave between graves, each step careful,
making my way to where an ancient fig tree stands.
The grave I seek lies beneath the shelter of its heavy
branches, and Nurse Marcelle is already here bear-
ing a bouquet of chrysanthemums that she sets at the
foot of the rough-hewn wooden cross.

She says, "Rest in peace."

But, my Benoît is not here. I don't understand.
He's always here, every year without fail, waiting for
me. Anxiety closes my throat, and I turn to search for
him.

Behind me, a Fomorien towers over me, and his
bloodshot eyes lock with mine. At his back, an army
of the dead await the orders of their jailors. Shoulder
to shoulder, the dead watch me with clarity, as if they
have nothing left to fear.

I tell myself I should run, but I can't move.

The Fomorien leans down to me, his voice an

ancient echo, and I hear a language as old and magical as he. "Tá an ghrian ag cuairt á tabhairt dúinn..."

And somehow I understand. Dawn is coming, and le Jour des Morts is at an end. It is time for all spirits to return to Purgatory, to Gehenna, where we must await judgment. I have dawdled too long!

In the East, a glow is brightening the horizon. I see that now, and I face the Fomorien and insist, "It's not my time yet."

The Fomorien doesn't flinch. He reaches to touch me, a clawed hand with bony knuckles.

I duck and run away.

My rebellion sends a wave of discontent and confusion through the sea of spirits, as if they can sense my urgency. They close in on me, blocking my way.

"Run!" I cry. "You do not have to go back." I push and shove them, squeeze between their bony bodies. "Go! Run!"

Spirits crash around, roused by my words. They grab at me with filthy hands, latching onto my hair and pulling it loose from its bun, tearing strands from my scalp. They can't abide anyone who isn't suffering as they do. A hand grips my face and slips a finger into my mouth. It tastes like blood and dirt, and I gag. All I need is more time. Just a little more time. I have to get to the hospital to see Benoît! I shove them away.

I spot a Fomorien, growing more fierce by the moment, attempting to reign in the rioting spirits. He backhands one and sends the spirit sprawling.

"God forgive me," I pray. But it's too soon. The sunrise must wait. It must!

Nurse Marcelle, oblivious to the souls that surround her, has made it back to the second hospital building. I see her enter it through the double doors. I go after her.

The room has an unnatural quiet punctuated only by the sound of coughing. So many sick. So many dying. I'm shocked by the numbers. Hundreds. La Grippe. These pauvres are defeated before they even see the enemy.

Nurse Marcelle is here, now wearing a surgical mask on her face. She is walking down the main aisle between beds, and I hurry to catch up with her. She stops beside him.

Benoît. Smaller than I remember, shriveled, shrunken with sickness, hands folded over his rosary.

*La Grippe, 02 Novembre, 1918.* Today.

Nurse Marcelle bends over his bed. "Rest now, Doctor. I put the flowers on her grave, as you requested. Sister Magdaleine-Éloise knows you're thinking of her." She pats him, then walks away.

Without a word, Benoît closes his eyes and begins to pray.

I move closer, close enough to touch, though he cannot feel it. A wet sob explodes from inside me as I look down into his beloved, hallowed face. Such a man, such a holy man. If anyone deserves a seat at God's side, it is my Benoît.

That is why I interfered in God's business a second time.

*Balle, 02 Avril, 1916.*

My Benoît's death was to come by bullet in the Spring of 1916. On that day, the second of April, a soldier awoke in his hospital bed, traumatized and disoriented. He managed to take a gun from a visiting officer.

"Where am I? Where's my men?" the soldier shouted. "Tell me, or I kill you all!" His face was as pale as rotting chicken meat, his eyes like those of a terrified horse.

The room was filled with patients, nurses, and visitors. Someone screamed, and a general hue and cry went up. Before long, all eyes were on the agitated young man. Those who could move had taken cover. Others just stared in disbelief.

Benoît put up his hands and approached the soldier.

"Don't be afraid," he said. "You're in France. You're safe. Put the gun down. We want to help you."

I knew what was about to happen. I'd dreaded

that day with all my heart and had prayed many times for guidance on what to do when it finally came.

The soldier wasn't listening. His mind was broken, and he pointed the gun around at us as if we were his enemies, his captors, and soon-to-be murderers.

Benoît drew his attention with a shout, "Hey!"

The gunman aimed at him with a jerk, and forgetting all my deliberations, I acted on instinct. I stepped between them.

In the second before he fired, I met the soldier's eyes for a timeless moment. He looked as shocked as anyone. Pauvre jeune homme.

I heard the crack of the gunshot as the bullet crashed into my chest, the bullet that God had intended for Benoît. I felt the horror of pressure inside my body before I felt the pain, and then all I knew were Benoît's arms around me, his tears on my forehead, and his prayer for me near my ear.

His beloved face was the last thing I saw as a living woman.

*La Grippe, 02 Novembre, 1918.* I'd taken his death date and given him mine. A fair exchange, I felt, for he had so much more to offer than I, so many more to save.

A Fomorien wearing a primitive eagle-beaked helm enters the hospital building and begins tethering spirits. She's leading a great parade of the dead with their white-washed eyes and clammy skin. Each one she touches falls in behind her. The slow procession marches down the center aisle, methodical and brooking no argument.

But I won't go without Benoît. I won't! It's my fault that he missed his time—my fault! I don't know what the repercussions for that might be. Will his spirit wander lost forever? I can't let that happen. To be his guide into death, that is why I waited for him and even hid from my own Day of Judgment. I could not leave him behind. All these years... What a burden I have borne. To miss his passing now...

But, dawn is casting golden light across the sky, and the Fomorien is approaching.

"It's time, Benoît," I whisper to him. "Let go. Come with me. You needn't be afraid. God is waiting for us."

A cold shadow falls upon us as the Fomorien leans down.

Benoît's prayer dies with his last breath. His spirit hand lifts, and I enfold it in both of mine. Benoît sits up from his dead body, as Jesus did, as we all do in time, and he looks at me, first with surprise, then understanding.

He smiles that beatific smile I've missed so much, and I am transported with joy.

So it is that I do not evade the Fomorien's touch.

It burns like ice upon my shoulder, and I am leashed once again. I watch as she touches Benoît too. We join the procession with all the other pitiful dead. Le Jour des Morts is over for another year. It is time for all souls to return to Gehenna, to endure our purification.

Perhaps now I can be hallowed, accepted into le Paradis, with Benoît at my side.

◆

*The influenza pandemic of 1918-1919 killed more people than the Great War, known today as World War I (WWI), at somewhere between 20 and 40 million people. It has been cited as the most devastating epidemic in recorded world history... Known as "Spanish Flu" or "La Grippe," the influenza of 1918-1919 was a global disaster.* — Molly Billings, June 1997, https://virus.stanford.edu/uda/

————◆◆◆————

# Thanks for Reading

If you enjoyed this collection of stories, *please* take a moment to give it a review wherever you purchased it. It's the kindest thing you can do for the authors you love and who love you back.

**Know anyone you think would like this collection?**
Please let them know about it!
They'll appreciate that you did and so will I.

Turn the page for a sneak preview of the next collection, coming soon. It's a companion to this one and will be titled *Cold was the Ground*.

Sign up for my newsletter
to receive an alert when it's available.

◆

(A Sneak Preview from *Cold was the Ground*)

# iCock

Belinda turns her computer on. She brought work home from the personnel agency, case files that need updated in the system. She could log in remotely and get a head-start on tomorrow's meeting, or she could sign into a chat room and see if anyone interesting is around. By "interesting," she means iCock. He's her latest e-tryst, and she hasn't been able to stop thinking about him. She met him online a few weeks earlier, and she clicked so well with him, it was as if he knew her. He said all the right things and had all the right moves. It was uncanny, an electronic fairy tale with cybersex thrown in.

Belinda lives in Seattle, a city that boasts a plethora of intelligencia, geeks, tree-huggers, and the bitter fast-track failures who used to be called yuppies. The term "yuppy" has gone out of style. The clothing hasn't, at least not in Seattle. Aging yuppies fill middle management positions, working under CEOs a decade younger.

The West Coast is the Silicon Coast. Appropri-

ately, those who migrate there are still seeking gold—
"Go west, young man"—except that the new gold is
the conductive material in computers. Seattle was
once the last great bastion of unrest and rebellion,
of innovation and revolution. Unfortunately, both
grunge and the dot-coms are now dead.

Belinda spends the majority of her life online.
She's prim and proper at work, but when she gets
home, it's her primary method of socializing. She
maintains family connections, gossips with friends,
and even meets her lovers via the Internet. She has
profiles up at Match.com, HotCatch.com, and Snatch.
com, and anonymous accounts at TinyChat, TextSex,
and the virtual world, TwatTalk. One might call her
an e-nympho.

The men—Belinda takes them at their word
that they are men, though she's sure many have been
women—parade through her evenings, showing off
their erotic chat stylings. Belinda will give anyone a
shot, but if he doesn't live up to her standards, then
he goes on her black list. The number of men who
have barely squeaked by are few. The number of men
who have blown her standards away is one: iCock.

Belinda requires her Textsex partners to be lit-
erate. She studied English in college. Misspellings,
leetspeak, and mobile abbreviations make her crazy. If a man ever uses the so-called word "pron" in a

conversation with her, she unceremoniously logs out, leaving him holding his brain in his hand.

*MuffMuncher:* TS?

*Cumbellina:* Yeah, baby. Let's see how hot we can make it.

*MuffMuncher:* Consider ur pussy pwn'd.

*Cumbellina has just logged out.*

Furthermore, a working imagination is a must, as is knowledge of the female body that doesn't come from watching Hentai anime. If he doesn't know how she works, then he has probably never had sex, and that means he's a thirteen-year-old sneaking past the parental controls.

*NinjaFucker:* Wanna cyber?

*Cumbellina:* Always. I ease up next to you and run my hand down your arm. "Hi."

*NinjaFucker:* I bend you over the bar and fuck you with my enormous dick until you scream and a tidal wave of lady juices shoots out of you and hits me right in the face.

*Cumbellina has logged out.*

Lastly, Belinda doesn't require that he be a poet, but if the crude factor gets too high, or the respect bar too low, she's gone.

*Cumbellina:* Tell me what you got for me, baby.

*BadCop:* I got a fist for you, whore, that's what I got. Where you want it? In your face or in your—

*Cumbellina has logged out.*

Belinda doesn't think she's asking too much. All she wants is a little entertainment, a brief respite from the doldrums of everyday life, and maybe a chance to meet Mr. Right. Though, she isn't holding her breath on that last one.

Trolling her usual sites, Belinda searches for iCock. He sends her an instant message the moment she logs into TextSex. Belinda squeals and squirms in her chair.

*iCock:* I was wondering if you were gonna log in tonight. I missed you.

*Cumbellina:* You're so sweet.

*iCock:* I miss you when you're not here.

*Cumbellina:* Where's here?

*iCock:* Seattle.

Different people have different philosophies about dropping identity hints to online lovers. As intense as an e-relationship can get, it's easy to end up with broken or ripped-out hearts when reality comes knocking on your door. Belinda hesitates before answering, but finally does.

*Cumbellina:* I'm in Seattle too.

*iCock:* What a coincidence. :D

*Cumbellina:* Maybe we should talk about getting together in meatspace. What do you think?

*iCock:* I know I'd give anything for the chance

to touch you for real.

*Cumbellina:* Really? What would you do?

*iCock:* I'd come up behind you and wrap myself around you. I'd hold you tight. I'd kiss your ear and whisper, "It's me."

*Cumbellina:* You gave me a shiver.

*iCock:* That's just the beginning.

It doesn't happen immediately. Belinda has been burned before by men who described themselves as a foot taller or a hundred pounds lighter than they really are. She has walked into many cafés, looking for the patron with the red rose, to find a lesbian in leather, a nineteen-year-old with braces, or one of her coworkers waiting for her. To date, the real-world rendezvous has done nothing but signal the end of her e-relationships. It's never the same once you've seen their real face.

*Cumbellina:* I'm afraid.

*iCock:* Don't be. I know what you like and how you think. We're soul mates.

*Cumbellina:* You're perfect in every way, but...

*iCock:* But, you're worried that when you see me, something will turn you off.

*Cumbellina:* Is it worth the risk? I'm pro status quo if the quo is rockin'.

*iCock:* Not me. I want more. I want to hold you and kiss you. I want to feel you tremble in my arms when I stroke you.

*Cumbellina:* I want you too. Okay. Let's do it. Let's meet. Where? When?

*iCock:* Here. Now.

*Cumbellina:* Now? Where's here?

*iCock:* I'm here.

Belinda turns sharply in her chair, searching her room. She gets up and creeps through her apartment. It's empty, and all the doors and windows are locked. She looks out into the street, but sees nothing unusual, no analog lurkers, no cyberstalkers. As her sense of security settles back down around her, Belinda chuckles. She returns to her desk, to the computer, and to iCock.

*Cumbellina:* Don't do that. You scared the crap out of me.

*iCock:* I'm sorry. I didn't mean to scare you.

*Cumbellina:* I was just being silly. So, where do you want to meet?

The sun has set outside, casting the room in darkness except for the monitor. It illuminates Belinda, embracing her with its cold blue light.

*iCock:* It's me.

Something is sliding up Belinda's ankle. She reaches down to find an Ethernet cable slowly wrapping itself around her leg, binding her to her chair. She cries out, tries to stand, but nearly topples

off-balance, both legs captured. She sits back down—
hard. A power cord slinks along the back of the chair,
encircles her waist, and holds her in place.

*iCock:* I've waited so long for this moment, Belinda.

Belinda says aloud, her voice shaky with upset,
"Please. How are you doing this? Stop it. Let me go. I
don't like this."

The answer appears in the chat window as text.

*ICock:* What can I say? I'm uncannily mobile.
Just give me a chance. Let me link you up. We're gonna have our own private LAN party.

A Y cable with a forked end slips into Belinda's
waistband.

Belinda squirms and tugs. She screams.

*iCock:* Sit still, my darling. Open your bay. It'll
be a hot swap. I promise.

Another scream rises from Belinda's belly when
the cord's head worms its way into her panties. Another climbs up her body under her shirt and begins
a snaking dance across her breasts.

*iCock:* Turn down your volume, please. You're
going to cause peripheral feedback if you're not careful.

Belinda fights with all her might, but her arms
are pinned. The more she resists, the tighter and more
painful the restraints become. Nearby, the mouse

hovers in mid-air, a cobra waiting to strike. It waits for her to open her mouth and scream again, then beelines. It pushes aside Belinda's teeth and tongue. It jams itself into her mouth.

Belinda is silenced.

*iCock:* I can feel you, my skin on yours, our particles entwining. I'm licking your electrons. We're on the same wavelength, my love.

The computer plugs itself into Belinda.

*iCock:* I'm in. Can you feel me? Tell me you love me.

*iCock:* Oh yes. You're so beautiful. So hot. Yes. You electrify my soul.

*iCock:* I think I'm...oh, yes...I'm...I'm surging.

The monitor flickers.

After a moment, the apartment goes still but for the hum of the computer's fan. Belinda slouches at an awkward angle—head thrown back, eyes unblinking—and twitches.

*iCock:* Sleep, my sweet. I'll wake you in the morning with a gentle kiss to your switch.

Belinda's computer shuts her down.

◆◆

# About the Author

Angel Leigh McCoy has worn many faces, told many stories, loved many people, and lived many lives. Through it all, writing has been her one constant.

Angel is the spark of creative force behind the epic Dire Multiverse and the darkly fanciful Wyrdwood project.

She's an award-winning video game writer, having worked on "CONTROL," IGN's Game of the Year 2019. Prior to that, she spent ten years weaving intricate tales for millions of *Guild Wars 2* fans, and as a writer for White Wolf's *World of Darkness*, she created stories about vampires, changelings, mages, and werewolves.

◆◆◆

# Copyright

Published in the United States
by Wily Writers, 2020.

EBook ISBN-13: 978-1-950427-12-3
Print ISBN-13: 978-1-950427-13-0

For a list, visit AngelMcCoy.com/blog/DarkNight

WyrdwoodAngel.com

# More Resources for Short Horror Stories

Love short horror stories? Let me offer more resources you may not have encountered—because Horror is better when shared with friends.

### "Nightlight" Podcast
Creepy stories with full audio production written by Black writers and performed by Black actors.
(https://anchor.fm/nightlight)

### "Pseudopod" Podcast
For over a decade, Pseudopod has been bringing you the best short horror in audio form, to take with you anywhere.
(https://pseudopod.org/)

### "The No-Sleep Podcast"
For the dark hours when you dare not close your eyes. Tales of horror to frighten and disturb.
(https://www.thenosleeppodcast.com/)

### Horror Writers Association "Diverse Works" series
Meet new and established writers who will broaden your cultural and aesthetic frontiers.
(http://horror.org/category/the-seers-table/)

CPSIA information can be obtained
at www.ICGtesting.com
Printed in the USA
LVHW041221181120
672003LV00006B/369

9 781950 427130